WILDFIRE RIDGE

WILDFIRE RIDGE

A middle-grade adventure novel

Mary Lee Soop
Emily Ullrich

This is a work of fiction. Names, characters, places, and incidents either are the product of the author's imagination or used fictitiously. Any resemblance to actual persons, living or dead, events, or locales is entirely coincidental.

Copyright © 2021 by Mary Lee Soop

All rights reserved. No part of this book may be reproduced or used in any manner without written permission of the copyright owner except for the use of quotations in a book review.

Book design by Emily Ullrich

ISBN 978-1-7373735-0-6

Published by Blackbird & Birch
www.maryleesoop.com

For Kim and Sandra O'Donnell, thank you for the encouragement, coffee, expertise, and laughter.

Contents

Chapter 1 1
   Martha

Chapter 2 7
   Blackbird Ranch

Chapter 3 20
   Mutant Blackbird

Chapter 4 28
   Evacuate!

Chapter 5 36
   Rescuing Princess

Chapter 6 40
   Saving the Ranch

Chapter 7 44
   Driving Out!

Chapter 8 49
   Into the Flames

Chapter 9 54
   Ouzel to the Rescue!

Chapter 10 60
   Run!

Chapter 11. 64
    Under Water

Chapter 12. 70
    We're in Trouble!

Chapter 13. 76
    The Final Push

Chapter 14. 83
    Ashes and Pain

Chapter 15. 87
    Waking Up

Chapter 16. 93
    Small Steps

Chapter 17. 98
    Aluminum What?

Chapter 18. 104
    The Surprise!

Chapter 19. 108
    Going Home!

Chapter 20. 116
    On Top Again

Acknowledgments 123
About the Author 124
About the Illustrator 125
Guided Reading Questions. 126

Chapter 1
Martha

"Aren't you the guy who fell down the stairs and broke your leg last year? Did they really call 911? Was the bone actually sticking out and is that really your blood stain on the bottom step?"

    It's seven thirty in the morning. I've had like four hours of sleep after a long night of gaming. I'm standing in front of my locker trying to decide if I need to keep my jacket with me or stuff it away. The new kid appears out of nowhere. She's bouncing on her toes and smiling so wide I can see the purple bands around each bracket of her braces. *Who are you?*

    I'm thinking about the Fortnite match I lost last night, so it takes me a minute to answer. "Yeah. That's me."

"I heard you got pushed by a high schooler."

"No, it was all me—the police report called it distracted walking."

"Oh, good." She sounds relieved. "I mean, it's not good that you broke your leg and all, but..."

"No, there aren't any rogue high schoolers roaming the halls waiting to pounce on us middle schoolers." *That could be a legit game concept.* "I'm Ouzel, by the way. Ouzel Lentz. It's like ooze with an 'L' at the end." I don't know whether to stick out my hand for a handshake or just nod my head. I do neither and just keep staring into my locker.

"I'm Martha. My Dad just bought a house up on Old Orchard Road. He works in Chico, but he loves the views and the quiet up here, so here we are."

She sounded way too excited about moving to nowhere. "I live on that road, too, but up on the very top—Blackbird Ranch."

"So, we'll ride the same bus?"

"Seems like it. I don't ride in the AM—my parents bring me. They're teachers at the high school in Forbestown." I decide to stop talking. Maybe she'll stop too and go to class.

"Cool. Do you know where room 203 is? That's my first class."

Great, now I've got to help her or look like a jerk. "Uh, it's just down there and around the corner. This place isn't big, you'll find it." I close my locker and pause. I have to walk that same way. What if she follows me and keeps talking?

"Well, nice meeting you. I'll see you on the bus, I guess." I turn and start walking down the hallway. She follows me like a lost puppy.

"Why were you distracted?"

"Huh?"

"You know, the fall? What distracted you? Did you have an out of body experience while you were falling?" She's walking right beside me. I feel her looking up at me, eager for a response. *Could this morning get any worse?*

"Uhhh, I was on my Switch. And no, I didn't die for a minute and float away."

"But video games aren't allowed in school."

"Who told you about it?"

"Everybody. They point at you and say, 'That's Ozzie. The boy whose blood is still splattered on the bottom step.'"

"Don't believe everything you hear. That stain is like a hundred years old. And the name is Ouzel, O-u-z-e-l, the 'ou' says 'oo' like in soup."

"Mutant, my man!" My friend Jake raises his hand to give me a high five. "Saw the leaderboard. You still got the most wins! Congrats!" He shoots air pistols as he walks past.

"Why did he call you that?"

"What?"

"Mutant?"

"Just a nickname."

"What's it mean?"

"Lots of things. Like I'm as tall as some of the teachers."

3

"It's 'cause a Mutant never dies." My other friend Julio sticks his head between Martha and me and butts into our conversation. "He's a legend, a thirteen-year-old mutant legend."

Martha looks confused, for a moment she's quiet. "Oh! Yeah, I heard you're a pretty good gamer."

I stop because we are in front of room 203. I turn to her and answer, "Yeah, I'm pretty good." I feel my cheeks heating up. "You play?"

"Only Minecraft. It's the only thing my mother will let me play besides little kid games. I gotta go in. See you later, maybe?"

"Yeah, sure." She pauses for just a second in the doorway. First day in a new school, in the middle of the year, that's rough. My grandfather always told me to encourage others, so I try to think of something. "Minecraft. That's a cool game. Don't be embarrassed by it."

Martha smiles and thanks me with her eyes.

I walk into my English class and see kids opening their laptops and tapping their keys. I feel the familiar dread of remembering that I've forgotten something important.

"What day is it?" I whisper to Julio.

"Thursday, in real life."

We have an essay due every Thursday that we upload at the beginning of class. I open my laptop to see how much I have already written. Maybe I can finish it now. I have the title and one puny paragraph. An excuse! I need an excuse to get Mrs. Chen to give me one more day.

The problem is that everyone knows everyone in this tiny town. It's hard to lie without being found out. You can't just say that your grandmother died or that your mom is sick. Everybody knows each other's business. Mrs. Chen walks in and asks that all essays be uploaded in the next 5 minutes. It's now or never. I walk up to her desk.

"Mrs. Chen?"

"No, Ouzel. No more excuses or extensions." She doesn't even look up. How did she know what I was going to say? "You've had plenty of time to turn in your essay." She looks at her screen. "And I see that everyone else was able to complete the assignment...on time. Ten points off for each day it's late."

I've used all of my extensions in this class, and it's only November. Must remember that. English—zero health. I'll have to write the stupid essay tonight.

"And," she says as she taps the cell phone basket. "Your phone." I take my phone out of my pocket and put it in the basket with the others.

I slump down in my seat. That's another thing I hate about this class. I don't like surrendering my lifeline. The laptops aren't any help. I can't access private accounts on them because they're school property. My friends and followers live all over the world, so there's always action going on. I need to take quick looks at Twitch and our Discord leaderboard so I don't fall behind. Casual gamers never get that.

Chapter 2
Blackbird Ranch

"I'm so excited to play Minecraft with a live person," Martha says as she plops down next to me on the bus. "Not that the online players are dead or anything, I mean they're not zombies..."

"I know what you mean," I say, hoping to stop Martha's stream of words.

"Thanks for inviting me over. I'm really excited."

"Sure." *Actually, my mom talked to your mom and invited you over.* "I've got to do chores first and then we can game."

"I know, I can't wait to help with the horses. I want to have my own horse. Dad says I can once we fix up the barn. When do your parents get home?"

"Not for a couple of hours. You'll have to go then, cause we have dinner and then I have to write an essay."

"Have a nice date, lovebirds," Jake says as he hops off the bus.

Martha's cheeks are bright red. I quickly try to reassure her. "Jake is always teasing. You'll get used to it."

Martha is weirdly quiet as we exit the bus and walk down the gravel driveway to the house.

"Well, this is it. The Blackbird Ranch in all her glory."

"Oh, I get it! Your username! MutantBlackbird. Blackbird is for the ranch."

"That, and because Ouzel is a type of blackbird. Want a snack?"

"I'd really like something to drink."

Martha follows me into the house. She heads straight for the pictures on top of the piano.

"Is this you?" She laughs picking up a framed picture. "You were so cute," she coos.

"If it's a little kid, then yes. I'm an only child," I call from the kitchen. Grabbing protein bars and bottled water from the pantry, I walk into the living room and hand one of each to Martha. "Here, we can eat on the back porch."

As soon as we step outside, I smell smoke. "Smell that? What moron is burning leaves when we're under a no burn order?"

"I like that smell. It reminds me of eating s'mores around

a campfire." Martha is smiling as she looks around the place. "No wonder Dad wanted to move us here. It's breathtakingly beautiful. Don't ever take this for granted."

"Never have, never will," I say as I stuff the last of the bar into my mouth. Martha still has half a bar left, but I can't wait. "You can stay here, but I've got to get started so we'll have time to game."

Martha crams the rest of her bar into her mouth, too. "Coming," she mumbles.

"Come on, ladies," I yell as I jump off the porch and run toward the chicken coop. I grab the feed bucket and shake it as I cast the feed on the floor of the coop. Squawks come at me from all sides as the hens frantically run home for dinner.

Martha squeals and backs up a few feet. "How many are there?"

I count out loud as each hen passes until I have all twelve safely inside the pen.

"Cool, you have twelve, so you get a dozen eggs each day."

"Sometimes. Not every hen lays everyday. Usually we get eight to ten eggs."

"Cool. I didn't know that. I have to warn you. I am pretty good at Minecraft. Well, okay, I am very good, actually." she says with a giggle.

This girl changes subjects so fast I've got whiplash. "We'll see. Let me round up the horses and then you can show off your skills."

"Yes, the horses!" She is squealing in a high-pitched voice.

"Umm, yeah. Just four. This isn't a working ranch anymore. Two of the horses are really old."

"But they're still horses! Yay! Do you ride them? Can I ride them? Do you have saddles?"

She's jumping up and down and clapping her hands. Does Martha have an off switch? It's like she's running on unicorns and glitter.

Martha follows me to the barn. I open the heavy doors, whistle, and wait. "Stand back," I warn Martha. "Amber and Jack like to race to the barn, and they won't stop until they reach their stalls."

"They're gorgeous," Martha exclaims as the two dark horses canter through the barn doors. Their hooves kick up a swirl of dust that causes Martha to cough.

"Thanks. They belonged to my grandfather Madjiki. He bought these two when they were yearlings. He wanted to breed them and start a Paso Fino training facility, but then he got sick and died."

"That's really sad. I'm sorry," Martha says as she walks into the barn.

"Wait," I tell her. "Look out there in the back pasture." I point to a white horse slowly walking toward the barn. "That's Princess. She takes her sweet time coming home."

"Wow, she looks magical! If she had wings, she'd be a golden Pegasus!"

"That's just the sun reflecting off her white coat. Wait until she's up close. You'll see that her best days are behind her."

"They're all gorgeous! I love them all. Can we go riding soon? Which one can I ride?"

"Uhhh, I haven't ridden a horse since I was like, eight. Maybe you could ask my mom and go out riding with her."

"Didn't you say four horses?"

"Yeah," I sigh. "Want to go for a walk? Grimey is probably all the way out in the back pasture by the fence, looking at the cars on the road."

"Looking at cars? Why?"

"Still looking for the old man's Jeep." I point to the far side of the barn where a tarp half-way covers a rusty Jeep. "Grimey was my grandfather's horse. Even though Grandfather Madjiki has been gone five years, that old horse still gets excited when he sees a Jeep. So, he likes to go and watch the road."

"Poor baby. He's lonely."

"You going to be okay walking through the fields in those shoes?"

"What's wrong with my shoes? They're what all the girls are wearing."

"Just not much to them, that's all."

"Guess I need boots, huh?" She says as she scratches her ankle. "And bug spray!"

Martha doesn't say anything as we walk carefully through the tall grass and around piles of decaying horse poop.

11

Finally, it's quiet enough for me to think. I make a mental list of what I need to do for tonight's Fortnite matches.

"Tell me more about your grandfather."

Martha's words sound like an annoying buzz. "What?"

"Your grandfather. Tell me about him?"

"I called him Madjiki, which means 'my man' in the Maidu language. Mom says that I claimed him as mine when I was like, two. My grandfather and mom are full-blooded first people from the Maidu tribe. I'm half Maidu."

"That's awesome. You should be proud of that."

"I am!" As we approach the boundary fence, I whistle.

"I can hear him. He's whinnying! Oh, sweet boy, come here, you precious thing."

"Come on, Grimey. Let's get dinner." Grimey lifts his head and nods his approval.

"He understands you!"

"Yep, first horse I ever rode."

All four horses go easily into their stalls. "It's only four o'clock. We don't usually feed 'em until five, so let's go in and get started."

"Awww, they look hungry."

"They can munch on their hay."

"Like an appetizer before dinner! We'll be back soon, guys," Martha says as she waves goodbye and blows air kisses.

"You know they're animals, right—not people?"

I pull out my phone as we walk back to the house. There are multiple notifications from Discord. *Oh, man! This isn't good.* I really need to get online and defend my lead, but Martha has made that impossible until after dinner. I hate it when real life gets in the way of my gaming life.

I turn on the TV and Switch. "Take a seat on the couch."

Martha is surprisingly good at Minecraft. I'd forgotten how much I like creating worlds with these block people. "I thought you'd play like a newbie, but you're really good."

"Told ya."

We're playing as a team which is way more fun than I expected. I'm in the zone fighting off skeletons when my phone alarm buzzes. "It's four thirty. I have to turn on the oven for my mom." I give myself a mental high-five for remembering even though there are at least four post-it notes scattered around to remind me.

When I get back to the living room Martha is looking at her phone. "Have you heard about this wildfire?"

"No, but we have them a lot this time of year. Don't worry. It's just life in Northern California."

"Duh, I'm not from a different planet. I'm from Chico. It's just that this one's really close."

"They've got a siren for evacuations. No worries until you hear that go off."

"We need to build a stronger fortress over here. I'll start with that, you may want to...Check your back, behind you!"

"Good eyes, thanks!" *Could Martha be better than me? No way, it's just my phone that's distracting me. Get in the game, Ouzel.*

"Can we pause so you can turn off your notifications? What's going on, with all that pinging anyway?"

"Sorry, it's just Fortnite updates."

"You must be pretty good if you're on the leaderboard."

"Watch out. Behind that boulder."

"Got it, thanks.

"I'm not just on the leaderboard. I was the leader." I shrug it off as no big deal, but it is a huge deal. I hope she's impressed.

Martha stops playing and stares at me. "In the world?"

"No, just the Northern California server."

"Oh, not even the whole state, huh?"

I'm working on it!

Mom's hand appears across the screen like a giant spider. That's the signal to get to a pause point and exit the game. *Glad I remembered to turn on the oven.*

"Hi, Martha. I'm glad you could come over. I'm Kuli Lentz," she says smiling. Her smile disappears and her eyebrows raise as she looks at me and asks, "Chores done?"

"Yeah."

"I helped him. You have beautiful horses."

"Thank you. You'll have to come ride someday." Mom turns her head toward me and drops the sweet smile again. "Ouzel, homework, done?"

"Yes," I lie. *I did some on the bus, and I'll finish that stupid essay tonight before I go to bed.* Martha gives me an elbow nudge and raises her eyebrows. "You're home early," I tell Mom, trying to change the subject.

"No, it's my normal time," she says as she walks out of the room.

"Play for fifteen more minutes?" I ask Martha.

"Sure, this is so much better than playing alone." The clicks of the controllers fill my ears and I am transported into another world.

"Use your potion on the Creeper!" I warn Martha.

"No, I can get him without using it. See?"

"You're right. You know what you're doing."

"We need to get out of here. Go right over that hill."

I hear the door bang. Dad's home early, too. Pausing the game, I call, "Dad, got a controller primed for you. We're almost finished, then you and me can play Rocket League."

"Maybe after dinner. Who is this young lady?"

Martha turns around to face Dad. "Hi, I'm Martha, your new neighbor. We bought the Cashwell's ranch."

"Nice, to meet you Martha. I'm Zack Lentz. I met your father in town last week. You're into gaming, too?"

"Just Minecraft." She turns around and helps me build another level to our fortress.

"Gaming is all this one seems to care about. Homework done?"

"Yes. Mom wouldn't let me play if it wasn't." I don't dare to look over at Martha.

"Horses in their stalls?"

"Yes. We rounded them up as soon as we got off the bus. Grimey was all the way out in the back pasture by the fence, looking at the cars again."

"Did Princess eat her oats?"

"Don't know. Haven't fed them, yet. It's not five. I'll feed them at five."

"Ouzel, it's after six. Where's your mother?"

"I don't know. In the barn? Kitchen? Six, really?"

"Oh Ouzel, I have to go. Mom has dinner on the table by six."

"I fed the horses," Mom calls from the kitchen. Her voice is stern. "Tomorrow, feed them earlier as soon as you put them in the stalls. Amber gets restless when she is hungry. She nearly kicked a hole in the stall door again."

Martha looks like she is about to cry. I don't know what to do so I blurt out, "Can Martha stay for dinner?" I look over to Martha. Her worried look changes to surprise. "We're having lasagna."

"Of course. We'd love to have you join us," Mom chimes in.

"Thanks! I love lasagna. Let me text my mom and see."

My phone vibrates in my pocket. I glance at it and see a video message from Jake.

"Go on and play it," Martha says from over my shoulder.

"Hey, Mutant, GoFer100 has just overtaken you!" He shows a screenshot from the Northern California

Fortnite leaderboard for most wins in Solos. I feel my stomach tighten. *Not for long, GoFer. Not for long. That's my spot!*

"What does that mean?"

"It means I have a long night ahead of me."

◆ ◆ ◆

Dad's already at the table staring at his phone which is unusual. Mom doesn't allow phones at the table. She carries over a steaming pan of lasagna. I feel the saliva ooze into my mouth.

"What does it say?" she asks Dad as she sits down.

"The fire's growing, but the wind is still pushing it northwest."

Mom twists a piece of her dark hair around her fingers. "That's no comfort. If the wind changes..."

"True, but it's still about four miles north of us. I'll call Five and see what he's hearing."

"Five is a nickname for Mr. Zhao, he's a friend of Dad's," I explain to Martha. "He was adopted from China on May 5th which was also his fifth birthday, and he has five kids so five is kind of his favorite number."

"Cool! My favorite number is 14."

"He has the ranch just north of ours and he's a volunteer firefighter. Been kept really busy this fall."

"We've had too many fires. Nothing scares me like wildfires." Martha lowers her eyes and she eats silently for a few minutes. Then she throws a mood switch and announces too happily, "This lasagna is extra delicious. Plenty of oregano."

Mom nods her head and smiles. "Grew it fresh this summer. Ouzel," Mom's smile disappears, "I got an email from Mrs. Freeman today." I almost choke on the hot lasagna. "She wanted to make sure I signed some papers she sent home with you."

I take a gulp of milk and try to think. "That was nice of her. Yeah, I think they're some permission forms and stuff like that. Nothing that can't wait. So, Dad, what direction is the fire moving?" I hope Mom's mind will switch back to the fire.

"If she went to the trouble of sending an email, then I need to see them tonight. Lay them on the front table." *Diversion tactic failed!*

"I think my mom got an email, too. It must be for the field trips." Martha gives me a quick wink. "Thank you for dinner, Mrs. Lentz. I need to get going."

"You're welcome here anytime, Martha. Ouzel, why don't you take Martha home on the four-wheeler?"

"It's okay, I can walk."

"No, it's after dusk. Ouzel will ride you down."

"Let's get going then." *I've got important stuff to do.*

"Thanks again for dinner. Nice meeting you both."

"I know you're in a hurry," Martha says as we climb on the four-wheeler. "Just take me to Rideout Road. I can walk from there."

"Are you sure?"

"Yeah, I like to walk at night and look at the stars."

"Here's a helmet. You can hold on to that bar. I won't go fast."

"Thanks." She looks up and sniffs the air. "I can still smell smoke."

We ride in silence until we stop at her road. I was expecting to be thanked for the ride. Instead, she grills me.

"Why do you lie to your parents about homework? And there is no field trip. Shoot, now I'm lying for you too!"

"I didn't ask you to cover me. It's my business, not yours. We're gaming buddies. All you have to worry about is watching my back in Minecraft. Not real life."

Lowering her eyebrows, Martha glares at me before turning and walking away. Gravel crunches under her feet as she disappears into the darkness.

I shrug my shoulders as I put the four-wheeler in gear. *She's annoying, anyway.*

Chapter 3
Mutant Blackbird

Mom is on the back porch when I get home. She stares at the sky and inhales deeply. "I can smell the smoke on the wind. I'm going to call the school and tell them I'm staying home tomorrow."

"Why?" I ask. If Mom stays home, then I have to stay home. I can keep up with gaming news at school better than I can under her eagle eye. "Mom, there are no evacuation orders. It's too soon. At least wait until tomorrow morning to decide."

"Wait until we hear back from Five," Dad adds.

Mom is super observant of fire patterns, so I expect her to argue. Instead, she slowly nods her head in agreement. But I can tell she's nervous from the way she twists her hair.

"I'll take out the garbage," I volunteer. Once outside I check my phone—lots of messages urging me to defend my place on the leaderboard. I feel my anxiety building. I look up to plead to the stars for good luck, but the stars look weird. Hazy circles surround each point of light. So much for star gazing, Martha. I sniff the air—it does smell like smoke.

"So, what's this game you and Martha were playing?" Dad asks when I come back in the house.

"Minecraft."

I'm heading towards the stairs when Dad asks, "Can you show me the basics?"

Really? Now? He sounds excited and I say, "Sure. I'll show you the basics." Plopping on the couch, I try to think of the fastest way to explain Minecraft.

"When did we get your first Xbox?" Dad asks. He knows the answer, it's just that he's kind of sentimental and likes remembering little details from the past. It's embarrassing and I don't have time for this.

"Christmas. I was eight." I can't help smiling as I remember feeling the electric bond form between my hands and the controller that day.

"There are probably souvenir corn chip crumbs still under the cushions. We played for days."

"Yeah, it was epic."

Dad really concentrates hard on my tutorial. "So, what do you think?" I ask, hoping he's not interested.

"Looks fun. Let's try a full game."

"How about tomorrow? I've played for hours already today."

"Hours?" Dad's eyebrows raise up and he looks at me over the rims of his glasses.

"Well, you know, not really hours. I wouldn't waste hours, but..." I'm saved by Dad's ringing phone. I listen carefully as I turn off the Switch.

"Hey Five, how's it going, man? Really, that rough? Kuli's thinking about staying home tomorrow. What's your take? Ah, okay. That's mighty kind of you guys. I'll tell her and Ouzel. Good night, brother."

The stairs creak as Mom comes down from the bedroom where she was grading papers and stands in the doorway. "And?"

"Five says to go on to school tomorrow. The fire is expected to keep on its path northwest. But, if the wind does shift and the fire starts to head this way, Five will call Jim to set the horses loose and drive to school to pick up the kids."

Mom nods her head in agreement. "Ouzel, promise me that when you get off the bus, you'll turn on the news and weather radio and listen for updates. And if they tell you to shelter at school, I'll come to you."

"Sure, okay," I respond as I take the stairs two at a time.

"Guys!" Mom says in her teacher's voice. "We need to review our wildfire plans."

"Too soon, Kuli. We'll review tomorrow night if the fire's still burning. We aren't in any danger right now and probably won't be. Dogs aren't barking up this tree." Dad picks up a controller before he realizes that the power is off.

I stop, turn around, and look at Mom's face. She's not backing down. Sighing, I come back into the living room. *Hold on GoFer. I'll get to you soon.*

Dad grabs his jacket, and throws me mine as we head out the door. The wind feels warm and dry on my face.

Why now, Mom? This fire isn't even coming in our direction. Mom hands me a garden hose as I walk through the barn door. "Go attach this one to the spigot by the back porch. Just leave it in a coil." I know better than to argue when she is determined like this. I do what she says.

Since I'm alone for a minute, I sneak a peek on my phone of a Twitch stream. I hope to learn a trick or two by lurking. As I walk slowly toward the barn, I watch a player glide down, do a sweet 360, and take out an unsuspecting enemy. A stupid rock trips me up and breaks my concentration. I look up and see a red glow in the northern sky. *Looks like The Storm is coming, but we're still in the safe zone.*

"Hey, Mom, anything else?" My pocket vibrates again, demanding me to get gaming. "If not, I'm going to go on up to bed."

"Put those papers on the table for me to sign before you go up," she says as she looks around. "There's a box by your door for your keepsakes...just in case."

I pull the math test with the failed grade out from my backpack. Beside the red score of 67 is a line for parent signature. I also pull out the proofs from this year's school pictures. I lay both on the table. Maybe seeing her sweet, baby boy will take her mind off the failing score. But I'm not worried. I'll study next time and pull it up like I always do.

Seeing the evacuation cardboard box just inside my bedroom door, I wonder what to put in it. *What is something that I can't live without?* There's one stuffed dog that I loved as a baby. It's not like I sleep with it anymore, but imagining it burning up makes me feel sad. I grab it from my closet shelf and throw it into the box. Madjiki's wallet and keys sit on my dresser, and I throw them in too. *There, I put stuff in the box to keep you happy, Mom.*

My eyes scan over my desk. This is what I care about—my gaming. The corner desk Dad built me is big enough for my laptop and two old desktop monitors. *Can't put these in the box, Mom.* I power up the PC tower that sits under the desk and bounce on the big, green exercise ball I use as a chair. *This is my happy place. This is true gaming.* "Okay GoFer, MutantBlackbird is here."

Glancing at the clock, I see that I have one hour before Mom and Dad come upstairs. They'll open my door and tell me goodnight. If I don't want trouble, I'll have the monitors off and pretend to be reading a book in bed. I set my phone alarm to warn me.

I bounce three times on the ball and crack my knuckles. My heart starts to beat faster as I open up Fortnite and put on my headphones. At this time of night, the wait in the queue is short. While I wait in the staging area, I see lots of players dancing and playing around. *Casuals. This might be an easy match.* The Battle Bus appears, and my palms start to sweat.

Lots of players jump out and start to glide down, but I wait. My eyes scan the landscape and I choose to jump out by an abandoned store. Spectators start filing in. The chat is blowing up, some cheering for Blackbird, but mostly teasing. I ignore them all. I land and start running for cover. I've got to find a weapon to protect myself and start searching for loot. Behind the service counter is a white tarp. Pulling it off is risky. I take a big breath and flip it away. I'm rewarded with a small green box—ammo. Under the drink machines I see a loot box. *Maybe, maybe!* Yes! I grab the weapon and run out of the store.

I'm staying away from firefights as I look for supplies. It's funny, but Five's talks about safety have gotten into my head. I try to hide from battle until I have enough healing items and shield potions. That's my strategy and so far, it's working.

It's down to two players and me. I'm hiding in the ruins of a tower when the headphones lift from my head. "I thought you were going to bed."

Mom's voice surprises me. I quickly close the game and turn on the ball to face her. The phone alarm is beeping. "I am. I just wanted to play a bit, you know, to wind down. See, I even set an alarm to remind me to go to sleep."

"I'm glad you're still awake, though. I'm feeling uneasy about this wildfire. You come straight home tomorrow after school and check the news."

"I will, Mom, you've already told me."

"If you see ashes, take the four-wheeler and get out. Don't be a hero and try to wet down the barn and house. It doesn't do much good anyway."

"Yeah, got it. Thank you!" *I've got to get back to the match. Leave me alone!*

"I signed the paper. We're going to get you a tutor. Dad's going to see who is available from the Math Department at Forbestown. Stop gaming and get to bed. It's a school night." Her tone means business.

"I will. Good night. Love you." I pull a pair of pajama bottoms from my drawer and start to take off my jeans. She's big on privacy, so she leaves quickly. *A tutor? I don't need a stupid tutor. I'll talk to Dad tomorrow and make him understand.*

I grab a towel and stuff it in the crack under the door. Escaping light can give me away. Turning off the desk lamp, I sit in the blue glow of the monitor. I put back on the headphones and turn down the volume.

The match I was in is over, I lost. *Darn it, Ma, I was so close—just two players left.* Just one more match, then I'll go to bed.

My shield is at 90%. I have two boxes of ammo and I'm well hidden. Two players were just taken out by GoFer100. *Thank you very much!* That leaves just him and me. If I can just be patient, then I might have a chance. My stomach is churning, and my hands are sweating. I decide to make my move. *The Blackbird is out of his cage!* I see movement on the corner of the screen, I turn and fire. *Take that, GoFer.*

I won! *That was epic!* I look down at my phone to see if I have time for just one more match. The display shows 2:06. *Oh, shoot!* I've got to be up in four hours. *How did that happen? It's that stupid GoFer's fault.* I close the game and power down the tower. Climbing under the cool sheets, I sigh into my pillow. *How can I sleep after that?* I get out of bed and put the laptop in the cardboard box—just in case.

Chapter 4
Evacuate!

"Now I see why you say we live in the middle of nowhere. Seriously, we ride the bus home for 45 minutes!" Martha sits uninvited by me after Jake gets up to sit by a girl he likes. "Do you know everybody in school?"

"Yeah. With only like a hundred students in the whole school, sixth to twelfth grade, it's pretty easy."

My phone pings. I tap on a video and see this sixth grader slipping on spilled soup in the lunchroom. The tray tilts and the soup sloshes onto this poor guy's pants. The video is slo-mo, and it's funny, but the comments are brutal. So, I add mine.

@TEOTD NBD SC

"What does that mean?" Nosy Martha asks.

"At the end of the day, no big deal. Stay Cool."

"That's nice of you to do that."

"Might soften the sting. I grew five inches over the summer and my name is Ouzel. I know about stings."

"But you seem so popular."

"Not really."

"What's that symbol you wear around your neck?"

"It's a word in Maiduan."

"What does it mean?"

"You could translate it as a summit, you know, like the top of a mountain. The one thing that matters most in your life that you spend your life climbing toward."

"Summit, cool."

"My grandfather Madjiki gave it to me. He never shared what his summit was, but I think it was making people feel better when they're down."

"That's what you just did, for the kid in the video."

"Yeah, I try, but my summit is gaming. It's what I'm good at."

"That's really cool, Ooze. Mine would be horses. Definitely horses. Want to Minecraft online when we get home?"

"Umm, sure, but only for about an hour. Remember, I have chores to do. And I'm Mutant or Ouzel, not Ooze."

"Not to me. You can do chores first, then text me when you're ready."

"The Fortnite Professional is going to play Minecraft with a girl. Ooh la la," teases Jake.

"Yeah, I am. What's it to you? Minecraft is a good game and I kick butt at it."

"Okay, okay, just kidding. Rocket League tonight, about eight?" Jake asks as he climbs down the bus steps.

"You got it," I say as I search YouTube for a greatest plays video.

"You kick what?" Asks Martha.

"What?" I shrug. This girl is starting to get on my nerves.

"Umm, last time I saved your butt from the Creepers, mister."

"I asked you to watch my back, miss." I can't think of anything else to say to her. She is sitting too close and is watching the video with me. *Who invited you?*

"What was it like being in the hospital?"

Talking to Martha is like switching games in the middle of a match. "Uhh, not bad, actually." I pause the video and look at her. She has dark eyes like Mom. "I was in bed for three weeks, so I got like ten hours of gaming in a day. Then when I was home, I was in a wheelchair for six more weeks. They sent a teacher to me from Forbestown, but it was only in the morning. So, I had all afternoon to game."

"That's why you're so good."

"I guess. Gaming got me through it."

"Didn't gaming cause it, too?" The bus stops in front of Martha's gravel driveway. "Text me when you're ready," she calls as she steps off the bus. "Hey look," she yells. I look out my window and see her pointing to large, billowing clouds of smoke on the horizon. *Pyrocumulus, cool!*

As soon as I'm off the bus, I head to the barn. Dropping my backpack by the door, I grab two bridles and leads. I might as well round up the horses and feed them now, so I won't be distracted while gaming. With the end of Daylight Savings Time, it gets dark early.

I whistle for Amber and Jack. My ears pick up rustling from the underbrush in the left pasture. Their manes and tails seem to float in the wind as they gallop to the barn door. I take a step back and open the double door wider. I can tell in their eyes that neither will pull up to let the other pass.

I pat them each on a flank and tell them to go to bed. Willingly they walk into their stalls and nuzzle the food buckets. "Start with this," I say as I throw in an armful of fresh hay. "More's coming." Jack snorts air out of his nose in protest.

Finding Princess and Grimey won't be as easy. They enjoy their freedom. I pull out the four-wheeler and fire her up. Since the other two were in the left pasture, I head out there. The air is hazy and it's getting hard to make out shapes in the distance. The wind picks up bits of sandy dirt and swirls it around in wisps. I go all the way to the property line fence and still don't see any sign of Princess or Grimey.

Pulling out my phone to check my time, I notice a message from Martha asking if I'm ready to play. I told her I'd only play for an hour. "Here's a gift for you, Princess," I call to the rolling hills. "One more hour of freedom, then it's in your stall." I push the four-wheeler into fourth gear and head for the house. Mom's porch flag is whipping around in this wind as if it's telling me to hurry home.

I unlock the door and head straight for my room.

Ready. I text Martha. *Signing in now.* I put on my headphones and wait. As soon as I hear her voice I say, "I'm going to fight an iron golem."

"Are you crazy? Those blockheads have tons of health."

"I'm feeling lucky."

I feel my phone vibrate in my pocket. I make a mental note to check it in a minute, but right now I need to stay focused. Martha is right. Defeating the iron golem will take skill and I don't want to fail.

"How are you going to defeat it?"

"I have the knockback enchantment on my sword, remember?"

"Ahhh, okay. What should I do?"

"Protect my back from zombies and skeletons."

And just like that, Martha disappears. "Martha," I ask through the microphone, "you still there? Martha?" I guess she had to go do something. The iron golem can wait until next time. I don't want to slay him without an audience.

I sign off Minecraft and open up Fortnite. After the high of last night's victory, I want to see if I can do it again. The staging area for this match is serious. Players are practicing their strafing and jumps. I crack my knuckles. *Focus, Blackbird. This could get dirty.*

My phone vibrates again. It's probably Martha apologizing for leaving Minecraft or Jake asking me to come over. I'll get back to them later. Right now, I have a bus to catch.

I gather my supplies and start building a tower. While I'm constructing, twenty players bite the dust. *My strategy is paying off.* Just as I'm closing the door to my fortress, an explosion rips apart all of my hard work. "No!" I yell and pound my fist on the table. My avatar falls to the ground and takes off running. Dodging in and out of buildings, I stay ahead of my pursuers. I stop, turn around, and jump over the head of another player. *Yes! The art of surprise.* I don't see the player behind the stone wall, and I'm hit. Just like that I'm out of the match. Not a win, but got a decent amount of experience.

I yank the headphones off and roll my neck. Checking the leaderboard, I smile. *Beat that score, you rotten rodent.* The room is dark, so I flip on the desk lamp. *Wait...it's too early to be dark, and why does it smell like burnt marshmallows?* In the distance I hear the faint whine of a siren.

I pull my phone out of my pocket. The first message is from Mom reminding me to turn on the news. *Darn it! The news. The wildfire.*

I slide down the long stair railing into the living room and turn on the TV. An updated evacuation map pops up on the screen. I move closer so I can see the detail of the purple shaded area. A weird muffled sound creeps into my ears. I know I should move. I need to act, but my body stays in one place as I keep staring at the screen. Our ranch is deep into the evacuation zone. The Storm is coming and I'm not in the safe zone. *What did Mom say to do?*

My phone rings and breaks my trance. "Hello!"

"Ouzel, this is Five. The wind has shifted and it's blowing the fire your way. Are you home?"

"Yeah, I'm here, but Dad and Mom aren't. They're still at school."

"You need to get out now."

"Can't I wait for Mom to get here?"

"They can't get up there, son. It's too late. Listen..."

"Can you or Jim come get me?"

"No. The fire has crossed Old Fork Road. You have to get yourself out."

"How? I'm scared, Five."

"I know, buddy. I am too. But we've got this. First, set the horses free, then—"

"Five, can you hear me? Five?" The call is dropped. I try calling him back, but it goes right to voicemail. *Did the fire take out a cell tower?* I tap on the second message from Mom.

Evacuate. Now! You know what to do.

When was this sent? Thirty minutes ago! I've wasted precious time. I've got to move. The wail from the evacuation siren is louder now. Thoughts are swirling in my head, but I can't catch one. *No, Mom, I don't know what to do. I didn't listen to your words because they were just worry words. They weren't important.*

I open the blinds in the kitchen and stare out of the north facing window. *Fire!* I can see the orange, flickering flames on our ridge—just a couple of miles from the house.

Chapter 5
Rescuing Princess

I imagine coming back home after the fire and seeing roasted chickens lying on the ground—little, brown mounds straight from the rotisserie. *Not happening to these ladies.* I open the fence around the coop and shoo out the hens. "Go, go, go." How do they know to head south—instinct? They run and jump in failed attempts at flying toward the main gate. *Ouzel - 1, Fire - 0.*

The horses. I've got to free the horses. I run toward the barn. The wind is blowing bits of dirt and leaves through the air. Amber whinnies as I open her stall. Her eyes are wide. She is either mad because her dinner is late or afraid of sounds that I can't hear. Swinging open Jack's stall, I yell at them to go. I follow them out and run to open the corral fence that surrounds the barn. "Haw, haw," I yell, "get out of here!" They both take off through the gate, running south—away from our ranch, away from the fire.

I feel a stab of sadness. Seeing them run away is like watching Madjiki's last dream be extinguished. At least Princess and Grimey are safe. They are out and can run… no…they can't. They're too old to jump the fences, and we are downwind from the fire. It will trap them against the fence line. They could get in the pond, but with this drought, it's only about two feet deep. They have to come this way to get out of the fences and run south. It's the only route to safety. *Do they know that?*

I grab the bridles and leads. I'm about to climb on the four-wheeler when I remember—apples! Princess can smell apples a mile away. I run back into the house and grab two apples from the fridge. *Always take supplies.*

I press the starter button and turn on the gas. The four-wheeler roars to life and then sputters and dies. I spit on the gas gauge and wipe a layer of mud off the glass. It's on E. *Why now?* No problem, just another challenge. *Think, Ouzel!* I look toward the above-ground fuel tank about fifty feet from the barn. It sits under a shed, so the sun won't heat it. A wooden shed. *That's not good.*

Five warned Dad about that. "If a fire ever reaches your yard, that wooden shed will act like kindling and lead the fire right to the gas tank." Gas will fuel the fire into an inferno. *Don't think about that. There are always bad things around me in Minecraft. Get the horses.*

I fill a gas can and lug it out to the waiting four-wheeler. My hair blows into my face and I brush it away. My skin feels gritty against my fingers. I look up and check for ashes. Nothing, yet.

The gears grind in protest as I push the four-wheeler into third gear too quickly. Because of the smoky haze, I'm afraid to go too fast. I suck in a big breath so I can call out to Grimey, but the air burns my lungs and I start to cough. *This is crazy. I'm risking my life for two old horses that aren't long for this world.* I ease up on the gas and squeeze the brake. Turning off the engine, I hold an apple in my outstretched hand. "Got an apple for you, girl." Within seconds I hear the gentle clop of Princess's hooves on the dry grass.

"Hey, girl. Where's your buddy, huh? Where's Grimey?" As I feed her the apple, I slip the bridle over Princess's head and clip on a lead. Turning my head toward the north slope I yell, "Grimey, here boy!" I try to whistle through my teeth like Madjiki taught me, but my lips are too dry.

Through the haze I see an outline of a person leaning against a tree. "Five?" I shout, but it's not Five. I know this person. The slope of the shoulders, the way he favors one leg when standing still. "Grandfather?" A cold shiver runs through my body. "Madjiki, is that you?" The figure disappears into the shadow of the trees. *Get a grip, Ouzel.*

A flash of orange light grabs my attention. A scrub tree bursts into flames up ahead on the trail. The horizon behind it looks like a pulsating, red backdrop from a movie set. "We're going home, Princess." I feel bad for Grimey, but Madjiki would want me to save myself. Wrapping the end of Princess's lead around the back roll-bar of the four-wheeler, I turn on the engine and slowly lead her away from the fire. "Princess, can you still trot?" I shout at her. I shift into 2nd gear and speed up. Princess begins to trot like it's nothing special. "That's it. Good girl," I yell over the engine.

Princess squeals and her eyes are wide with fear. "You're right. Time to run." The handle is warm under my palm as I turn the accelerator. The four-wheeler speeds up and Princess starts to canter. She finds her rhythm like she was a young mare.

"Come on barn. Where are you?" I scream. I've read about horses running so hard that their heart explodes. I don't want that to happen to Princess.

The barn suddenly appears through the smoke and I ease up gently, so Princess has time to adjust her gait. I untie her lead and guide her to the open gate. As soon as I slide off her bridle, she bolts and gallops into the haze. *Be safe, girl! I'm sorry, Grimey. I'm so sorry. Ouzel - 2, Fire - 1*

Chapter 6
Saving the Ranch

I've got a choice. I can wet down the house and barn and try to save our home, or I could leave and head south on Old Orchard Road. The horses and chickens chose to leave, but as Madjiki used to say, "I've been given intellect, tools, and opposable thumbs to get things done." I'm staying put to fight this fire.

There are four hoses—one on each side of the house. I run over to one and turn the spigot to the left. I squeeze the nozzle handle and a stream of water gushes out. *Where do I start?* I remember Five telling me about making a fire break perimeter. If I can take away just one of the things fire needs, it will die. Water takes out the heat, so I choose to wet the yard around the house and barn first. *Embers. That's the enemy.* Scanning the sky, I see tiny ashes and smoke, but no glowing red embers.

I stand about ten feet from the house. *How long did Mom say to do this?* I spray water on the lawn for three seconds. "One-one thousand, two-one thousand, three-one thousand." I lift my arm as high as it will go and direct the stream to the roof. My arm sways left and right as water starts to drip down into the gutters.

Five also told Dad he should replace this shingle roof with a metal or tile one. "Hot embers can melt little holes in the shingles and set the plywood underneath on fire. Embers can't do that to metal." Dad agreed, but we didn't have the extra money. *It's okay, Dad, I'll keep this old roof from burning.*

I walk in a wide circle wetting down the house and yard. It takes time, but I think it's worth it. Walking toward the barn, I pull the hose as far as it will go. I feel a sting on the back of my neck. I swat at it like a mosquito. At least the barn has a metal roof, but the sides are wood. I start spraying down the walls when I feel another sting on the top of my head. The air gets hotter and starts to burn my nose as I breathe. Looking up, I see what looks like fireflies fluttering in the smoke. *Embers!*

Dropping the hose, I run into the barn. *Think! You've been in tight spots lots of times.* I've got to get a filter for my face. Five always stressed that. *Protect your airway, son. You can't help others if you can't breathe.* Running to the tack closet, I open it. I look for the stack of face mask filters and safety goggles we use when we fill the silos. *Don't want to get feed dust in your lungs, son.* I grab a mask and put it over my nose and mouth. *Don't want to get hot smoke in my lungs either, Dad.* Grabbing two more masks, I stuff them into my back pocket. My eyes are already watering, so I put on the goggles, too. *I wish shield potions were real.*

I step out of the barn and freeze. Smoke is coming off our porch roof like someone built a campfire on it. *My house is going to burn down.* This truth hits me like a punch in the gut. Grabbing the hose, I scream, "No!" at the fire. I keep screaming like I'm in a battle as I spray water on the hot spot until the smoke dies down. *Ouzel - 3, Fire - 1.*

I run around the house checking the roof for smoldering embers. I don't see any, but I feel another sting on my arm. Five always wears a heavy, fire-proof coat when he is on the job. Running up the porch stairs, I push open the door and head for the closet. I find Mom's yellow, slicker raincoat with the hood. It's the closest thing I've got to fire gear.

Reaching under the coats, my fingers find the bag where we keep the winter hats and gloves. Hats and scarves fly behind me until I find my winter gloves. I try to put them on, but they're way too small. Dad's leather gloves might work. I pull them on, but they're too big and bulky. My fingers won't be able to grab anything in these. Mom's leather riding gloves are on the floor beside me. I'm wearing her coat, might as well try on her gloves. The leather stretches skin-tight over my knuckles as I tug. These will work.

The boxes. The cardboard boxes with our keepsakes may stand a chance if they're in the barn. I take the stairs two at a time and grab the box by Mom and Dad's bedroom door. Their box is full and too heavy to carry under one arm. I look down and see images of a baby Ouzel staring at me. These mean everything to Mom. I grab Madjiki's wallet and keys from the box by my door and toss them into Mom's box. I balance my laptop on top of my baby picture and lift. Carrying the heavy load in my boney arms makes me breathe deeper and I begin to cough. *Go, go, go!* I've got to get to the barn. Running down the stairs and out into the yard, I expect to reach cool, fresh air, but the air is worse...much worse.

    I stumble through the barn door and scan for a safe place to put the box. No place seems safe. Putting the box down on the bare dirt floor, I lean over it and pant. *Think! What would MutantBlackbird do when faced with this? He would... I would... use a tool or use a life or...* "This isn't a game," I yell to the empty stalls. "I don't have extra lives or health or superpowers. It's just me." Tears burn my eyes. I've lost.

Chapter 7
Driving Out!

I look up through blurry tears and the smoky haze. Inside the open tack closet, I see Dad's two-way radio tucked into a space on the bottom shelf. He uses it with Five when they're hunting or when the cell signal goes out. Dad says it works for up to 35 miles, so maybe, just maybe, Five has his radio on his belt and turned on. I reach out and grab it. I pause just a second before flipping it on. This is my only chance. If no one answers this message, then I am all alone in the middle of a wildfire.

    I push the power switch up and hear static. That's good! The batteries work. Pressing the transmitter button, I yell, "Hello, hello, can anyone hear me?" I release the button and wait. *One-one thousand, two-one thousand, three-one thousand.* Nothing. I try again. "Hello, this is Ouzel. I'm at the Blackbird Ranch. Over."

The radio crackles and I hear my name. "Ouzel, I hear you, son. Where are you?"

"Five!" I can't believe it. I'm talking to Five. Just hearing his voice makes me feel like I'm still in the fight. "I'm in the barn. I sprayed down the barn and house and the horses are free. Over."

"No, no, no...listen to me. You can't ride this out. You've got to get out. Over."

"I know. Should I use the four-wheeler? It's gassed up. Over."

"Yes, use the four-wheeler. Get on and ride as fast as it will take you down Old Orchard Road. Grab some horse blankets, the thick wool ones, and throw them around your shoulders—at least two. Go, now, and don't stop. Over."

"Got it. Over."

Running into Princess's stall, I grab the blanket that we put over her at night. I think it's wool. It feels itchy like wool. I hold it to my mask and breathe in horse instead of smoke. *I hope you made it, Princess.* I don't even want to think about Grimey.

I run to the opposite end of the barn where Grimey's stall is holding another thick blanket. Grabbing it from the rack, I start back toward the four-wheeler. I turn my head to look at Madjiki's Jeep one more time. The Jeep has been sitting under that tarp for years. *Try it.*

I stop. *This is crazy. It can't start. But, what if...*

Running to the Jeep, I pull off the tarp with one tug. I throw the blankets in the passenger sheet. *Ma's box.* Sprinting back to the front barn doors, I scoop up the box and the two-way radio and return them to the jeep like I'm in a relay race. As I run, I hear my grandfather's keys jiggling against the box. *Okay Madjiki, I need your help.*

The smoke is getting thicker and I can hear the crackling and popping of flames from outside. I push my hand to the bottom of the box. My fingers close around the feather from Madjiki's keychain. I grab it and jump into the driver's seat—his seat. My feet touch the pedals easily! I stick the key into the ignition. *Pump the gas to prime the engine.* Madjiki always pressed the gas pedal down three times, so I do the same. *Please start, please start.*

I turn the key. The engine sputters and dies. *Help me, Madjiki!* Turning the key again, I give the engine more gas. With a shudder, it turns over and hums as if it was started yesterday. I can hear Madjiki's throaty laugh in my head. *Thank you, but now what?*

I need to open the doors at this end of the barn. The Jeep idles as I raise the two-by-four that holds and locks the two doors together. It's heavier than I thought, and my arms shake as I struggle to lift it up and off its brackets. I push open the doors and scream from the blast of hot air in my face. The grass and trees are on fire about twenty feet in front of me. *I've got to get out now.*

An old push mower and my forgotten bike are parked in front of the Jeep. I shove them out of the way toward the flames, but the helmet—that I can use. I push my bike helmet onto my head, but it only goes down half way. *Stupid growth spurt!* Scanning the walls, I see Dad's bike helmet dangling from a nail to the left of the door. I pull it over my ears and jump into the Jeep. Wrapping the rough horse blankets around my shoulders, I fold the loose edges under the seat belt straps and grab the wheel. This jeep has no doors which I used to think was cool. Now, not so much.

I push the stick into drive and freeze. The flames from the tree line are snaking toward me. My foot won't move from the brake to the gas. I just keep staring at the flames like I'm hypnotized. I can't move. My heart is pounding, and my ears feel like they are plugged with cotton. *Move, Ouzel!* This is what it means—paralyzed by fear. I am paralyzed. *I'm not a mutant. I'm a scared kid.*

Chapter 8
Into the Flames

Crackling static is coming from the radio. I look over to the box in the seat beside me. My right arm moves, and I pick it up. Five is calling my name, but the signal is weak and keeps breaking up. "Ou… zel…Ouzel…" Hearing Five call my name breaks the spell and I drop the radio in my lap.

I make a low guttural growl in my throat as if I'm an animal about to strike. Taking my foot off the brake, I press the gas pedal down. The Jeep lurches forward toward the flames. I turn the wheel hard to the right to go around the barn and toward the main gate. An ember falls on my exposed knee. It quickly burns a hole into my jeans. I frantically slap the hole with a corner of the blanket as I steer toward the gate. I turn my head and take one more look back. The roof of our house is on fire. Wetting it down didn't help. It just cost me time.

I turn right onto Old Orchard Road. I want to speed up, but I can only see the road for a few feet in front of the headlights. Technically, I've never driven a real car or truck. I drive the four-wheeler and digital cars in games, but now that it's real, I don't know what I'm doing. I ride on this road every day, but I've never paid much attention. I'm usually on my phone or Switch.

This part of the road is gravel with no lines that reflect light. My eyes look for a point in the center of the gravel and try to stay there. The embers coming at me make it look like I'm flying past stars at hyper speed. *That's it Ouzel. You're doing it.* I remember Madjiki's words when he taught me how to ride a bicycle. He was so proud. If I make it through this, he'll be even more proud. *Can you see me, Madjiki? Wherever you are, can you see me?*

The right side of the road is glowing. I thought the fire was only behind me, but it's to the side of me, too. The red light from the growing fire is freaking me out and I start to feel dizzy. *Breathe, Ouzel, breathe.* Attacking an iron golem is nothing. I am driving a jeep through a wildfire. *Wish Martha could see this!*

I realize that the flames are helping me to see. So far, the fire is only behind me and on my right, and is still about twenty feet from the road. But that won't last, not with this wind. With the embers flying, the other side could ignite at any moment. *Go, go, go!*

An explosion erupts behind me. I look back and see a column of orange flames and thick black smoke lift above the treeline. *The fuel tank.* That's it for our house and barn. I press down on the accelerator just as a hunk of metal from the tank crashes on the hood of the Jeep. It rolls into the windshield and leaves a small nick as it flies off onto the road. Spider lines slowly crawl from the center of the nick and spread across the glass. *Don't shatter, please don't shatter.*

    I pass Martha's driveway. It's on the right, where the fire is burning. I hope she got out in time. Were we just gaming a couple of hours ago? I feel like this is a bad dream and that I'll wake up soon. A glowing ember lands on the thin space between my glove and sleeve. The sting on my skin reminds me that this is real, very real.

    I glance at a tall pine tree up ahead. The fire is wrapping around it like a rope. The flames are alive. That's what Five always tells me. They are breathing and eating and moving. My eyes stare at the burning tree for too long.

    When I look back at the road, there's a big rock sitting in front of me. It's too big to hit straight on, so I swerve and go off the road. Screams fill my ears and it takes me a moment to realize that they are mine. The Jeep leans left as I ride over the dry brush and small trees. Branches reach in and scrape my cheek. A large pine sits in the middle of my path, so I turn the wheel hard to the right and try to get back on the gravel road. The front tires find the gravel, but the back tires spin on the dead leaves. *Take your foot off the gas.* I ease up off the gas and the tires slow down, finding some traction. The Jeep is back on the road, but my stomach is in my throat.

The road makes a sharp curve, so I slow down and try to stay in the middle. As I round the bend, I see flames devouring trees on both sides of the road. "No!" I yell. I feel more angry than scared. *You will not win.* I try to go faster, but I can't. The smoke is just too thick. If I go off the road on either side, that's it—no extra lives in the real world.

I hear a loud crack above me. I duck my head as if something is about to hit me. *Speed up!* I push the accelerator to the floor. The Jeep lunges forward just as a burning tree falls behind me. I feel the gust of wind hit me from its impact with the ground. I want to look back, but I'm afraid I'll run off the road. *Just keep pushing forward. Don't stop.*

It's getting harder to breathe. I slow down so I can steer with one hand. I yank off the mask and hit it against my knee. Maybe it's getting clogged up with ash particles. I look down quickly and see that it's black. I reach into my back pocket and pull out a clean mask. I slow down even more so I can use both hands to pull off the helmet and put the mask's elastic bands over my head. I rub the goggles with the edge of the horse blanket. That helped. I can see and breathe better, so I speed up.

There's a slight bump as the Jeep leaves the gravel and gets on the smooth pavement. *Finally!* I feel relief for only a second. I take my foot off the gas and press the brake. This is worse. The pavement has no lines or reflectors.

The black pavement reflects the red glow from the flames. It looks and feels like I'm driving on fire. It's hard to tell what's pavement and what's burning ground.

There's a dark shape lying across the road ahead of me. I pull up to it slowly and stop. It's another smoldering tree. Only this time it is in front of me. I'm trapped.

Chapter 9
Ouzel to the Rescue!

I'm going to die. I lean over the side of the jeep and throw up. As I rest my head on the steering wheel, a memory flashes into my brain of Five teaching me about fire holes. There are these holes or trenches that firefighters dig to crawl into to escape from wildfires. I look around in the jeep for a shovel or something. The jeep is empty except for Mom's box and the radio. There's not even a jack or a spare.

Grabbing the radio, I press the send button. "Hello, Hello?"

"Ouzel! I am glad to hear your voice, son. Been worried about you. You alright?"

"No, Five, I'm not. I'm on Old Orchard near where the pavement begins. There's a downed tree blocking the road. I'm trapped." Hearing Five's voice makes me cry like a little kid.

"You're still on Old Orchard?" Five's voice changes. He sounds worried. "It's okay, Ouzel. The four-wheeler should be able to get over that. Just—"

"I'm not on the four-wheeler. I'm in Madjiki's Jeep."

"The Jeep! What the heck are you doing? You don't know how to drive!"

"The Jeep started up and I thought it'd be faster. Help me Five. The fire is on both sides of the road now."

"Listen to me, Ouzel. That Jeep has four-wheel drive. You can probably drive right over that tree. How big around is it?"

"Not too big. About the size of my thigh, I guess."

"Great. I want you to put the Jeep in reverse and back up enough to give yourself room to build up speed before you drive over it."

"But I can't see behind me. I'll run off the road."

"The tail lights will glow red to help you see."

"Five, the whole road is glowing red!" I push the shift to reverse and gently press on the gas. I look up at the rearview mirror, but I can't see anything, so I try the side mirror. I can just make out the edge of the pavement. I use that as my guide as I back up until the road starts to curve. My hands are shaking as I grab the radio. "Okay, I did it."

"Good job, son. Now accelerate and drive right straight over that thing."

I'm distracted by smoke near my right eye. One of the horse blankets is smoldering on my shoulders. I pull it off and throw it in the seat next to me. I half stand so I can press

55

the gas pedal to the floor. The tires squeal and I fall back into the seat. Holding the wheel steady, I close my eyes and head straight toward the tree.

There is a strong jolt, and just like that, I'm on the other side of the tree. I don't know what four-wheel drive means, but it works, and I am back to battling this fire. *You haven't won yet.*

"It worked, Five, it worked!" I yell into the radio.

"Yes! You did it, son! Now just stay in the middle of the road and drive. You're going to be okay." Five sounds excited and relieved. He believes I'll be okay, so I do, too.

The flames are only on my right again. That makes me feel better. The blinding, red glare on the black road is only on the right, too. I can see the dark edge of the pavement on my left, which makes steering easier. I try to go faster.

"Ouzel!"

I take my foot off the gas and slow down. Keeping my eyes on the road, I feel blindly for the radio on the seat beside me.

"Yeah, I hear you."

"Can you talk and drive at the same time?"

"I don't know. No, not really." The Jeep swerves slightly. I need two hands to steer straight.

"It's alright. Just lay the radio down and listen. There's a man with me down here who's looking for his wife and daughter. Wants to know if you know them. Last name is Malkovich. Daughter is your age. Name's Martha. Have you seen them? Answer when you can."

I slow down and reach for the radio again and press the send button. "I know Martha, but I haven't seen her since we got off the bus. Talked to her earlier while we were gaming."

"Just be on the lookout. They'd be in a red Range Rover."

"Got it." *I hope they got out.* "Five, where are you?"

"Just outside of town where Old Orchard meets Highway 13. We've set up a fire break. Get down here and you'll be okay."

I start to speed up again when the headlights catch movement. I ease off the gas and see a wild hare on the side of the road. It's not hopping for its life. Instead, it's barely moving. I catch the reflection of its eyes as it looks straight toward me. Madjiki didn't appreciate these pesky creatures eating his garden, but he would never set traps or put out poison. *They're part of this life, Ouzel. They're trying to make it in this world just like us.*

I stop the Jeep, climb out, and run up behind the hare. "It's okay, little fella, I'm here to help." The hare doesn't move as my hands encircle him. His fur is hot, and his heart is beating a mile a minute under my fingers. I put him on top of the scorched horse blanket. He's as still as a statue except for his blinking eyes. "Hold on, fella, we're going to fly."

I get the Jeep up to 45 mph. It really does feel like we're flying, but then I see two red, glowing circles ahead on the road. My stomach and throat tighten. Not again!

I'm afraid that I'm seeing another fallen tree or worse–fire burning the road. I press on the brake and try to figure out what I'm seeing through the smoky haze. I put my hand on the radio, ready to explain the obstacle to Five.

Taillights! That's what they are! Taillights. There's a car stopped on the road in front of me.

Chapter 10

Run!

I step on the brake and stop with a jerk. In front of me is the red Range Rover. *Why are they just sitting there?*

Unbuckling the seatbelt, I throw off the horse blanket. I take off the helmet, so if it is the Malkovich's car, Martha will recognize me. My face feels gritty and hot, and the air mask must be totally black by now. She still might not recognize me. I jump out of the Jeep and sprint to the driver's window. I bang on the darkened glass with my fists.

I hear a high-pitched scream as the passenger's door opens. "Ouzel!" Martha shouts. She gets out and runs around to the driver's side and opens the door. "Mom, it's okay, this is my friend Ouzel. His dad will know what to do."

Mrs. Malkovich doesn't even look at me. She's staring straight ahead. I turn my head to see what she's seeing. The road is blocked. Not by one small tree, but by a huge tree that is burning. There is no way the Jeep can drive over that monster.

"It's okay. I have a radio," I tell Martha and her mom. "I'll ask for help." Martha nods, but her mom just sits there staring at the burning tree.

"Where's your dad?"

"Probably where your dad is. In town waiting for us."

"You drove that Jeep? In this?"

"Yeah, but I don't know what I'm doing. Hold on." I press send and start talking. "Five. I found the Malkovichs. Over."

"Copy that. Are you still on Old Orchard Road? Over."

"Yeah, the bottom half. We're almost down, but we have a problem. There's this huge tree blocking the road. It's too big to drive over and it's on fire. We need help. Over."

"Ouzel...listen...me." The transmission is breaking up. "Your position...Old... Road...surrounded by fire. No help..."

Martha stares at me. "What does he mean, no help?"

"It means we're on our own. We need a shovel. Do you have one in your car?"

"How would I know? We have suitcases, some food, and probably a spare tire, and a jack."

"We need to dig."

"There's no time, Ouzel!" Martha looks around and waves her arms at the fire on all sides. "Maybe if we get in the car and just wait..."

"No! The fire will burn us like kindling. I'm not giving up!" Walking to the back of the Range Rover, I open the back hatch and start looking for anything that I can use to dig.

"What do you—"

"Shh!" I hold up a hand to interrupt her. "Listen." In the distance off to my right, I hear a whinny. I turn and stare into the burning woods. Beyond the flames is the outline of a horse with a concave back. "Grimey?"

"There's a horse! See?" yells Martha pointing into the flames. I'm glad she sees him, too. That means it's real, and not just my imagination.

"We have to help him," Martha cries. Grimey stares straight at us, then turns and runs down a small hill away from the flames. Even with the crackle and pops from burning wood, I hear a distinct splash.

"Water," Martha and I yell together.

"Get your Mom out of the car. We're running towards that water."

"Are you crazy? We can't run through the flames. We'll get burned."

"We'll get burned if we stay here. Do you have any blankets?"

"I'll check." Martha opens the driver's side door of the Range Rover and starts to talk to her mom.

Running back to the Jeep, I grab the horse blanket that is still on my seat. As I put the helmet back on my head, I see that my arms are speckled like a Dalmatian. Mom's rain slicker has small round burn holes scattered all over it. These embers will ignite Martha and Mrs. Malkovich's clothes. I have to get these blankets around them, now. *Darn, the hare.* Without thinking I pull the hare off the blanket by the extra skin on his neck. My button-down shirt is still tucked into my pants from school, so I stuff the hare down the front. He squirms for just a second and then sits still. Its ears stick out from the top of my shirt and tickle my chin as I run toward the Range Rover.

"Here, hold these over your heads and around your bodies. We're running straight through there," I explain as I point to the burning trees. "Then down the hill where there's a pond of water. Don't stop, just keep running and dive into the water."

"I can't," says Mrs. Malkovich. *Come on, lady. You're the grown-up. You should be telling Martha and me what to do.* She's frozen, just like I was earlier.

"If we stay here, we will die. We have to run, now!"

"Mom, come on," Martha pleads. "I won't go without you."

A scrub bush by the left side of the vehicles bursts into flames. We are now surrounded. Martha screams and takes off running into the flames toward the pond. Mrs. Malkovich jumps out of the car and follows her as I bring up the rear.

Chapter 11
Under Water

The fire line isn't very wide. I count twelve strides and I'm out of the flames. My feet are hot, and I wonder if my shoes are smoldering or maybe even melting. I keep running and zigzagging between the trees.

Splash! Hearing Martha hit the water is better than having a five game win streak. The pond slowly comes into view through the haze, and I see Mrs. Malkovich standing by the bank looking at the water. She is bent over and coughing like Madjiki used to do. As I run up to her, I see that the blanket over her shoulders is smoking. Pulling off the blanket, I push her into the water. She comes up sputtering and calling for Martha.

"Mom, I'm here!" Martha swims over and hugs her.

I feel bad for pushing someone's mother into a pond, but that smoking blanket scared me. "Are you all okay?" I ask as we tread water. Even though it's dark, we can see each other in the red glow from the fire.

"I think so. My feet are stinging really bad," Martha says.

"So are mine. And look." I hold up a hand to show how much I'm shaking. There's a sudden lurch in my shirt followed by a terrific sting. "Owww, what the—" I yell.

"You have a rabbit in your shirt!"

"Actually, it's a hare," I explain as I struggle to get the scared creature out of my shirt while kicking my legs and trying to keep my face above the water. With a push from his powerful hind legs, the hare leaves the safety of my shirt and jumps into the water.

"Cool, I didn't know hares could swim. Look at him, he's so cute." Martha's voice is a high-pitched squeal again.

"All mammals can swim if they have to." I look down at my chest. Four long scratches go from my waist up to my collar bone. Blood is starting to seep into the ugly red welts. I gasp and a part of me wants to cry, but of course, I can't. Not in front of Martha.

"Where is he going?"

"He better not hop back into the fire after all I've done for him." We watch through the smoke-filled air as he swims to shore and starts furiously digging near the bank.

"Look, he's digging a fire hole! Hurry, buddy." The fire is all around the pond now. In a matter of minutes, it will be at the banks.

"Thank you, Ozzie," Mrs. Malkovich says. "You saved our lives."

"It's Ouzel, Mom, not Ozzie."

"No problem. It's a weird name." I wanted to tell her that it means Blackbird, but an ember lands on Martha's head. "Go under," I shout. She looks at me like I'm speaking Martian. I reach over and push Martha's head down.

"Why did you do that?" She sounds mad as she comes up blowing water out of her nose.

I quickly point to her mom. "That's why!"

"Mom, your hair is on fire! Dunk under!" This time it is Martha who pushes her mom's head under.

"If the embers touch us, they'll burn us," I call out. I look around to see if there is any shelter nearby, but of course, there isn't. Grimey is in the middle of the pond with just his nose out of the water. He is completely still, so he must be able to touch the bottom.

"Let's get to the middle." I figure animals have an instinct about how to save themselves. We all start swimming towards Grimey. "Martha, get your head under and just come up for a breath." The ashes and embers are starting to fall like rain.

I take a deep breath of smoke and air and go under. I swim blindly toward Grimey. My hand bumps into his side and I surface. Grimey has that wild, scared look in his eyes. He is snorting air in and out too fast. If he panics, he could bolt. I need a blanket to cover his eyes. Neither Martha nor her mother have the blankets on them anymore. I threw Mrs. Malkovich's off near the bank.

"Martha, can you hold onto Grimey's neck and sing to him? He likes country songs and that might calm him down. And here..." I take off the helmet and place it on her head. "... you can keep your head above water and sing. I'm going back to the bank for the blanket."

Martha wraps her arms around Grimey. "I don't know any country songs!"

Mrs. Malkovich starts singing Rafi's *Down By the Bay* as I swim underwater toward the bank. My scratches sting like crazy as my arms make heart-shaped patterns. As soon as my knee scrapes the gritty bottom, I surface. The blanket is scorched and smoking, but it's still there. As I grab it and push it under the water, I see a quick movement in the corner of my eye. I turn to see the hare's tail disappear into a hole in the bank. "Be safe," I call after him.

Swimming with a wet, wool horse blanket is like swimming through pudding. The embers hitting the water give off bursts of steam which makes it hard to see and breathe. My muscles are quivering when I finally reach Grimey. I drape the soggy blanket over his ears and eyes.

"His neck muscles are relaxing. I can feel it!" Martha croaks.

"Get your head lower. Breathe in the air that's right above the water."

"Let's all hold on to Grimey. I'm freezing," Mrs. Malkovich instructs through her chattering teeth. I realize that I'm cold, too. The water didn't seem this cold at first, but the longer we're in it, the colder it feels.

Wind is swirling over the pond and lifts a spray of water into our faces. *The fire is creating an updraft.* The flame line has reached the banks of the pond from two sides now. The fire should jump the pond and continue on its path of destruction. I'm scared because I don't know what to expect. Will the pond water heat up or will the fire suck up all the oxygen?

"Stay low," I yell to Martha and her mom. "The worst is coming."

Chapter 12
We're in Trouble!

Martha is holding on to Grimey's thick neck, her mom is standing by his side with her arms around Martha, and I am by his rump. Only Grimey's head sticks out of the water, until we humans tilt back our heads and expose our noses for air. Mrs. Malkovich is right, Grimey's body is warm. *Thanks, Madjiki, for sending him.*

    I wait for the water to heat up, but it doesn't. I expect that the next breath will be harder, but it isn't. The wind is hot and fierce, but we're doing this. Go under until my lungs beg for air, tilt back and lift with my toes until my nose finds air, suck in a full breath and go back under. I count each rep until I reach 29.

    "Ooze! Look!"

I bring my head out of the water and look around. We're behind the flame line. The ground around the pond is smoking. Ashes are still falling, but I don't see any red embers.

Martha points to the bank. "Look, burning bushes." Small foothill pines are being gobbled up by the flames, but the worst is downwind from us.

I'm about to celebrate when I hear splashing from the left bank.

Martha shrieks, "What is that?" The splashing is followed by the sound of swimming. "Can mountain lions swim?"

I'm about to call out because I figure the sounds are from other people. But Martha's words stop me. I rip off the goggles and squint my eyes to see through the smoke. I can make out hazy shapes. "Definitely animals, not people, and there's more than one."

"Mom!" Martha sounds really scared which makes me scared. "What if they're panicked, hungry mountain lions?"

"Shhh, don't imagine problems. Mountain lions would have outrun the fire. Whatever is coming is more scared of you than you are of it."

Finally, Mrs. Malkovich is talking like a grown-up. I'm ready to let her be in charge.

Grimey whinnies. He must smell the invaders. I hope he's sending out a friendly vibe.

"Deer!" Martha exclaims. "Three, no four!"

She's right. Four deer are swimming calmly toward us.

Grimey whinnies again. The lead doe swims right up to him and sniffs his nose. The others swim right by us as if it's normal to see humans in the middle of a pond. Grimey shakes the blanket off his head. He lurches forward and starts swimming with the deer.

"Hey boy, come back!" *Don't leave me!* Grimey swims off to the opposite shore from where we entered. Maybe he knows something we don't. "I think we should follow him."

"Martha!" screams Mrs. Malkovich.

I look around, but only Mrs. Malkovich is beside me. We both go under the surface frantically feeling for Martha. Her floating hair tickles my hand. I grab a handful and pull. Mrs. Malovich gets her hands under one of Martha's arms. Martha's eyes are closed when we pull her to the surface.

"Take off the helmet," Mrs. Malkovich orders.

As her mom holds her up, I unbuckle the helmet. The top of it is speckled with burn holes. "What's wrong with her?"

Mrs. Malkovich tilts Martha's head back. Martha takes a breath and starts to cough. "I'm just so tired, Mommy. I can't tread water anymore."

Martha was holding on to Grimey. When he bolted, she went down.

We need to get her to the shore. Mrs. Malovich starts to swim the lifeguard side-stroke as she holds up Martha. I feel like I should help, but Mrs. Malovich seems to be doing okay. I swim beside them toward the bank, the deer, and hopefully Grimey.

As we get closer, I see the outline of Grimey and Madjiki waiting for us. All the cold seems to drain out of me. It's weird, but I feel warmth and love. All I want to do more than anything is to hug Madjiki, but his outline fades into the smoke. Grimey snorts and whinnies as we get closer. I want Madjiki, but Grimey will do. I reach up and give him a two-armed hug around his strong neck.

Grimey is standing in about five inches of water. I look at the once muddy bank and see why. The mud is dry and cracked. Red hot embers are scattered among smoldering tufts of burnt grass. I look around for the deer, but they're gone.

Dad decided not to shoe Grimey anymore–he's too old and he doesn't walk much—except for today. His sole and frog can probably feel the heat. "We'll just wait here," I whisper to Grimey.

"We have to get Martha out of the water," Mrs. Malkovich demands.

I cup my hands and splash water onto the cracked bank. The water hisses and evaporates into steam. I keep splashing until the ground starts to soften. "I think this spot is cool enough." To check I put my bare hand on the ground. "It's safe."

We pull Martha up on the bank and sit her down on the cool spot. She's shivering all over. I remember Five saying that wet wool holds in heat. I look around for the wool, horse blanket, but it's nowhere. *Probably at the bottom of the pond.*

"Mom, my feet really hurt," Martha cries.

Without the light from the flames, it's really dark. Mrs. Malkovich bends down and gets close to Martha's feet.

"Here, my phone is waterproof, so maybe..." I take out my phone and swipe the screen. The screen looks weird—all pixelated. I know where the flashlight icon should be, so I press that spot. The white light flicks on. "Yes! Here," I say as I hand Mrs. Malkovich the phone.

She shines the light on the bottoms of Martha's shoes. "Let's keep your feet in the water. That will help the heat and pain. You too, Ouzel. Feet in the water."

"We can start walking soon and Martha can ride Grimey." I feel relieved, like the worst is over. I'm warmer just from getting my body out of the water. The air is still heated from the fire, but I don't know for how long.

"Let's rest here and let the ground cool." Mrs. Malkovich hands me back my phone. The phone is way too hot. I try to press the spot to turn off the light, but it goes out on its own. *My phone is dead.*

Mrs. Malkovich starts talking in words I can't understand. "What is she doing?" I whisper to Martha.

"Praying."

"What language?"

"Hebrew. We're Jewish."

"Can she pray for me, too?"

"Of course."

I feel better after the prayer, and Madjiki feels close by.

Mrs. Malkovich starts to cough again. I watch her shadow bend over as the coughing takes over her body. We need help, and soon. "We have to keep moving."

Martha tries to stand up. She screams and sits back down. "My feet!"

"It's okay. Your mom and I can lift you onto Grimey."

I try to help Mrs. Malkovich lift Martha onto Grimey, but my skinny arms aren't strong enough. Martha is coughing and shaking. After three tries I state the obvious, "I don't think this will work."

"You're right. She can't ride your horse, not like this."

Martha lets out a moan and starts to cry even harder as she sits back down. I don't know what to do or say to help. "Maybe…you can…drive out," she says as her cries turn into hiccups. "It isn't too far…back to the car."

"Martha, there is no more car. There may not even be a road."

Chapter 13
The Final Push

"I can ride Grimey down to the firefighters base camp. I'll get help…"

"Ouzel, it's dark and we don't have any light," interrupts Mrs. Malkovich.

"I can go back to the road and just follow it to town. Horses can see in the dark better than humans." *I am not spending the night out here, lady.*

"I think you were right when you said there might not be a road. A wildfire can melt asphalt, Ouzel."

I put a hand on Grimey for balance and lift my foot. My shoe is there. I feel the bottom of it but only touch wet sock. The run through the burning forest must have burned holes through the bottom of my shoes.

Martha takes in a deep breath and starts coughing. It sounds bad. Five told me a story about a guy who survived a wildfire but then died of pneumonia because of smoke inhalation. My own lungs start to hurt just thinking about it. I feel my back pocket and pull out a wet, but clean mask. I hand it over to Martha.

"Here, see if this helps."

"Thanks, but I think it is too late for that."

"Mrs. Malkovich, I have to try to find that road and head to town. Our lungs may be okay for now, but they won't stay that way. We breathed in a lot of smoke and hot air. I think we all need a hospital, not just Martha."

"You're right, but you can't go. Not yet. It's too hot. Look." She nods towards the south. There is still smoke coming from the ground and the trees are dropping glowing limbs. "Let's wait. Thirty minutes. Let the heat escape from the ground and road."

We can't wait thirty whole minutes. I feel the ground near the pond. It's no longer hot, just comfortably warm. I step out of the water and feel nothing. My feet are numb. I pull on Grimey's mane and lead him out of the water, too. "Hold up, boy."

I don't like waiting, especially in a dark, burned-out forest. I'm scared and cold and I don't know what to say. Martha is sucking air in through her teeth like you do when you're in pain.

"Martha, I'm going for help." Before I can get my leg over Grimey, it's my turn for a coughing fit. I read somewhere that this guy actually coughed up a piece of his own lung. I feel like that's what I'm doing.

"No!" Martha screams. "You can't leave us." With every breath she takes, I hear a wheeze.

"Ouzel, honey, I don't think it's safe for you to ride Grimey. What if he collapses?"

"Grimey is 28. He's a Morgan and they've been known to make it to 35."

"Will he let you ride him?"

I stroke Grimey's strong neck. "Yeah, I know he will. He's here to take care of us."

Mrs. Malkovich starts to cough and I hear her spit out phlegm. Martha moans and lays back on the ground with her eyes closed.

"Grimey will get me to town. The firefighters will know where this pond is. Just hold tight." I'm surprised at how calm I sound. I'm not sure Grimey can get me to town. I'm not sure I can ride in the dark at all. What if the fire break didn't stop the fire and the town is burning, and I'm heading back into it?

I whisper into Grimey's ear. "One more ride, old boy." I haven't ridden bareback since I was about eight. But…I'd never driven the Jeep before and I did that.

I grab Grimey's mane and swing my leg up and over his back. He whinnies and turns his head to stare at me. "I'm sorry, old one. But I need your help." *Guide him down, Madjiki.*

I nudge Grimey's sides and we set out. I pull his mane

and try to get him to go back to the road, but he refuses. He starts walking straight, following the deer's trail.

"I'll be back, I promise," I call to Martha and her mom.

"Wait," Martha calls out. Grimey stops. I hear Mrs. Malkovich walking toward us.

"Here, put this on," she says as she hands me the helmet.

Grimey plods through the forest. He must be able to see because he goes around trees and steps over branches. I hear rustling in the underbrush around us. Critters are probably peeking their heads out from their holes. The forest is coming back to life.

I feel a rattle in my chest as I breathe. I don't have asthma, but Jake does, and I've heard his rattle before. I take a breath and force myself to cough. A slimy wad of mucus comes up in my mouth. I spit it out, but the rattle is still there. "Come on boy, faster."

Five told me that after he's been in smoke, he makes himself cough up the phlegm. He explained that our lungs surround the particles of smoke and ash with mucus. The problem is that if you don't cough that junk up, pneumonia can set in. I wonder why Grimey isn't coughing. *Do horses cough?*

I pat my leg and feel the familiar rectangle in my pocket. I pull out my phone and touch the screen. Nothing. I push both volume buttons to do a hard restart. After dropping two phones into water—one in a water pail and the other in the toilet—Dad decided that he needed a waterproof phone. He didn't want to look like he was the only one who needed the protection, so Mom and I got new waterproof phones, too. But I don't think the phone was meant to be in smoke and heat and dirty water.

The phone's dead. No phone, no laptop, no PC, no Switch, no house, no barn…the reality of loss hits me. I start to cry like I did when Madjiki died. Grimey stops and looks back at me. He nibbles my knee with his lips. "Kisses won't help this time," I tell him.

I can't stop now for a pity party. I can't. I click my tongue and tell Grimey to go. The slow, bumpy sway of his gait is comforting, like sitting on Mom's lap as she rocked me when I was little. My crying makes more mucus and I wipe my nose on what's left of my sleeve. Every few seconds, I cough and spit. My sides are aching and I am so thirsty. I try to lick my lips, but they are swollen and sore which makes me cry harder. Suddenly, Grimey stops.

"What's wrong, boy?" I wipe my eyes and stare into the darkness searching for flames or anything that might have spooked Grimey. I see nothing. I hear nothing except for Grimey's snorting and my ragged breathing. My body is shaking and I realize that I am spooking Grimey. *Get a grip Ouzel.*

I close my eyes and try to calm down. I think of the day Madjiki died. Everyone was around his bed holding hands just like he wanted. My whole family, plus Five, in one room. I remember feeling warm and happy even though I had to say goodbye to my Madjiki. Mom and my Uncle Coe told stories about Madjiki—stories I'd never heard before. There was a lot of laughter and just a few tears. When it was over and he had passed on, we stayed in his room and sent prayers up with him. I felt love in that circle.

    The circle is still here. I can feel it. The love from my family covers me even in this cold, dark forest.

    My crying and shaking stops. "I'm sorry, boy. I'm okay. Let's go." Grimey snorts and resumes walking.

Chapter 14
Ashes and Pain

Grimey picks up his pace. We're out of the forest and in a field. There are glowing embers and small fires scattered around and I'm worried about the soft frogs of Grimey's hooves. *Maybe that's why he is trying to trot.*

Up ahead I can see a row of round circles of white light bobbing up and down. I keep staring as I try to figure out what I'm seeing. Grimey is almost at a canter and it takes both hands to hold onto his mane.

People! The lights are the headlamps on the firefighter's heads. They're beating down the last of the flames with their shovels. "Five," I try to shout, but after all that coughing, my voice is only a soft croak.

Several guys lift their heads and point toward us. I think they're shouting, but voices are muffled inside the helmet. Grimey barrels toward the line of firefighters. I see the line break as the guys step back. Grimey's back end rises and pushes me into his neck. *He's jumping!* Grimey jumps over the smoldering fire line. We did it. He did it. We're out of the fire!

I slide down Grimey's back and into Five's arms. He pulls off my helmet and hugs me tightly. His headlight blinds me for a second as he looks at my face.

"I need an ambulance, over here," he motions to someone behind me.

"Why? I'm okay, but the Malkovichs aren't. They need the ambulance."

"Your lips are blue, buddy. You need some oxygen."

"It's just ashes. I'm fine." *I'm Mutant.* "Martha's feet are hurt really bad and Mrs. Malkovich is coughing worse than me."

"Where are they?"

"Straight through the woods that way," I point behind me. They're on the south—" I'm interrupted by a long series of hacking coughs, "—bank of a big pond. It might be the one on Jake's property. I can show you."

"We've got this, Ouzel. You go with Kee to the hospital."

"No, I can't…leave…Grimey!"

"I've got him, Ouzel." I turn to the familiar voice and see my Uncle Coe. I never realized how much he looks like Madjiki. He comes over and gives me a bear hug just like Madjiki used to do. "I found Amber and Jack, too. I'll take them back to my place," he says as he points to his horse trailer.

"They're safe? Look out for Princess, too."

"Don't need to. She came running into our corral hours ago."

Kee Chen puts a blanket around my shoulders. "I'll tell your folks to meet you at the hospital," Five calls to me as Kee helps me step up into the back of the ambulance. *Oh man, that essay.* Kee is Mrs. Chen's husband.

Kee hands me an oxygen mask and I hold it over my nose. The stream of air coming from it smells like cotton candy.

"Take some deep breaths and then I'll buckle you on the gurney." I try to breathe deeply, but the coughs won't let me. I yank off the mask as Kee hands me a spit pan.

The gunk from my lungs is black. I look up at Kee, trying to find some reassurance.

"Put that mask on and sit over here." I hesitate for a second. The gurney has a clean white sheet on it. I am filthy dirty, but I lay on it anyway. Kee attaches a belt across my lap and one over my knees. He's about to press sticky pads on my bare chest when his eyes widen.

"What happened to you, buddy?"

I pull up the oxygen mask. "Wild hare. I saved it."

Kee is smiling and shaking his head. "Do you know when you last had a tetanus shot?" He tries to place the pads so they don't touch the scratches.

"Last month."

"Oh right. Halloween." Kee is laughing now. "You're one lucky guy. Must have a guardian angel watching over you."

Wires with clips on the end that look like tiny jumper cables clip onto the pads. Kee flips a switch behind me and I hear a whirring sound.

"Ouzel, you in pain anywhere, besides your chest?"

"My ribs hurt some, but it's my feet that hurt the most." The siren begins to wail and the ambulance lurches into motion.

Kee moves down to take off my shoes. I'm about to ask him to tell his wife that I lost my laptop. Maybe he can convince her to give me more time for the essay.

Searing, burning pain takes over my left foot. I rip off the mask and scream. The pain takes my breath away. I try to push out my abs and force air into my lungs. Something's wrong. *Julio is wrong. This mutant can die.*

Chapter 15
Waking Up

Someone or something is pressing on my chest. I raise my hand from my side and try to get it off. My hand meets another hand that is pressing hard on my chest bone.

"Here he is! He's waking up."

"Ouzel! It's Mom. Can you open your eyes?"

Of course, I can open my eyes. My eyelids feel so heavy. *Just five more minutes.*

The pain in my chest returns. *What is that?* This time I force open my eyes. "Quit it." I push the hand away.

"Hey, buddy. Welcome back," Dad says.

Where did I go? My throat is sore, and it hurts to talk, but I have so many questions. The top half of the bed slowly rises. Mom offers me a cup of ice water with a bendy straw.

The cool water feels fantastic on my throat.

"Why am I in the hospital?" I whisper.

"Do you remember the fire?"

Why would I forget the biggest thing that's ever happened to me? "Yeah!"

"You needed to have a tube down your throat to help you breathe. Just so your lungs could heal. It was easier to keep you asleep for a few days while your body healed," Mom explains.

"A few days. I've been asleep for three whole days?"

"Actually, this is day four."

I've lost four days? But, it feels like I was only asleep for a short nap! Now I understand what FOMO means. I shake my head to try to understand when I remember. "How's Martha? And Mrs. Malkovich?"

"Same as you. Getting better. Five found them right where you said. You saved them, son." Dad's voice is breaking up. "I'm proud of you."

"Are they here, in this hospital?"

"Right down the hall."

"Can I go see them?"

"Sure, but not right now. Maybe tomorrow."

"How are the horses? And the chickens? Did you find the ladies?"

"Coe says the horses are settling in. Grimey had some burns on his feet, but he doesn't seem to be bothered by it. The chickens hopefully found a new home. We haven't seen them."

"Dad, I'm sorry about the Jeep, the house and barn. I tried to save them."

"It's just one of those things, son. The fire was too fast and hot. There was nothing you could do. It was you we were worried about."

"I could have left earlier. Mom, I didn't go right in and check the news." I looked down at the white bed sheets. I couldn't look Mom in the eyes and see the disappointment. "I went up to my room to play Minecraft with Martha. Then a match of Fortnite. By then it was too late. The flames were at the back property line." I twisted the sheet around my fingers. "I grabbed the boxes you wanted. They were in the Jeep with me. I just…left too late. I'm so sorry." Using a corner of the sheet to wipe my eyes, I confess, "I really messed up."

"Yes, you did, Ouzel. Your actions almost took away the thing I treasure most. I was so afraid I had lost you."

"I'm your summit?" I look up and into her brown eyes.

"Yes, you and Dad." Mom takes my hand and puts it over hers. She reaches for Dad's hand and puts it over mine. "You once said that your summit was gaming. Is that what you want it to be? Think about it," she says gently as she kisses my head.

"Mom and I are going to leave you alone for a bit, so you can rest."

My parents walk out of the room and close the door.

They never yell or stuff like that. She speaks the truth and then leaves me alone to think. Usually, I don't think. I just act like I do—to please them.

What is my summit—the one thing that means life to me?

◆ ◆ ◆

A guy dressed in Spiderman scrubs brings a tray of food for me. "Sorry, kid, only liquids for now." The tray has a cup of hot brown stuff on it that must be broth. There's a bowl of red jello squares that smell like fake cherries. *Great—gourmet dining for me!* I taste the broth and it's very savory. I never knew plain broth could taste this good.

There's a knock at my door. "Come in," I croak.

Jake peeks his head in. "There he is. I knew the Mutant would rise out of the ashes!" Jake walks in carrying a helium balloon that says, "It's a Boy!"

"Hey!" I give him a weak fist bump as he sits down on the edge of my bed. I move my feet to give him more room. I'm either wearing really thick socks or bandages. It's hard to tell.

"How are your feet? That's gotta hurt—burns on the bottoms of your feet. What were you doing? Running through the flames?"

"Yeah, actually, I was."

"Whoa! Really? I didn't hear that part."

"What did you hear?"

"Just that you were missing. Then once you were found..."

"I found the firefighters," I interrupted. "I got myself out."

"Then they said you had lung damage and burned feet. Julio told people your feet were burned off."

I laugh, but I wiggle my toes just to be sure. "I'm okay, but our place is toast."

"Yeah, so is ours. We hope to go back up tomorrow and look around. I'll send you a video of it."

"Thanks, but I'm totally offline."

"Dude, that's, I mean, I'm so sorry. But, hey, the Blackbird will fly again, right?"

"Sure. Someday. Sorry, but I'm feeling kind of dizzy."

"No probs. I'll try to come back tomorrow. I'll bring my laptop."

"Thanks." I lower the bed as Jake leaves. I close my eyes just for a minute.

Chapter 16
Small Steps

"Ouzel, breakfast is here." Mom is tapping my arm.

"Can I have pancakes?" I ask before I open my eyes.

"Once you're home. Let's see what surprise they have under here." Mom helps me raise the bed and sit up straight.

"We don't have a home," I remind her.

"We're staying at Coe's right now. Home is where we're all together."

"Where's Dad?"

"At school."

"Why aren't you there?"

"I'm taking some time off to be with you." Mom lifts the tray cover. "Look, solids!"

Yellow scrambled eggs and greasy strips of bacon sit on a white plate. I usually can't eat greasy food for breakfast, but I'm so hungry. "They're good, really good," I say as I shovel the eggs into my mouth.

A nurse comes in to check on me. "I'm Susan," she says with a smile. "I'll be taking care of you today. How about getting out of this bed?"

"Yes, please." I push back the food tray and pull back the covers.

"Not quite yet. I need to remove your catheter and then the Physical Therapy crew will come in to get you up." She takes my temperature and blood pressure, "Looks good. I'll be right back."

"A catheter, again?" I moan.

"You've been asleep."

I look under the sheets. *This is embarrassing.* "Why do I need Physical Therapy?"

"The soles of your shoes melted into your skin, leaving severe burns on your feet. Standing on them may be painful. And, you haven't walked in five days. Your muscles are going to be weak."

The eggs and bacon feel heavy in my stomach. The thought of more pain scares me. I reach for Mom's hand.

Nurse Susan comes in and with one quick pull the catheter is out. "Think you can sit on the side of the bed and dangle your legs?"

Of course. I sit up and move my legs back and forth.

"Is this good dangling?" I'm trying to be funny, but my heart starts pounding and I feel like I'm going to throw up. "I'm going to be sick," I announce. Mom takes my hand and presses the skin between my thumb and forefinger.

"Just breathe. Your body is adjusting to being upright."

A big guy comes in with an old person's walker. *Is that thing for me?*

"Ouzel, remember me? Big Ed?"

"You grew a beard!" It's the same PT who helped me recover from my infamous broken leg.

"That I did! Got to admit I was surprised to see you back here again. I like you man, but next time, let's catch up over burgers! You know the drill. I'm going to buckle this strap around your waist. It helps me hold you up if you start to fall." *I won't fall.*

"Okay, Ouzel. Let's try to put some weight on your feet!" Nurse Susan sounds too happy. *Yay, I love feeling pain.* "It's going to hurt like having someone touch your sunburn."

"I've never had a sunburn." Her enthusiasm for my pain is getting on my nerves. I put my bandaged feet on the floor. I slowly put weight on my right foot. "It's sore, but not as bad as I thought." I try putting weight on my left foot. "This one hurts more. It stings."

"Your left foot was burned more than the right."

"Put your hands on the walker and push up to standing," Big Ed says. "That's it. Now shift most of your weight from your legs to your arms and to the walker."

"It's not so bad," I tell Mom. "Walking with the brace last year was worse." I try to take a step. I wobble, but I feel the pull from the strap around my waist.

"Excellent, my man, Ouzel," Big Ed says. I remember how encouraging he was. "Let's walk four steps up, turn around and walk four steps back."

My arms are quivering and my heart is racing, but I'm walking. Turning around is tricky because my left foot can't support much weight. "I feel like an old man."

"You look like an old man," Big Ed laughs.

Laughing feels good. My ribs ache when I laugh, but I keep laughing. It's better than crying.

"Okay, want to try out your wheels?" Big Ed helps me sit in a wheelchair. "If I remember right, you were a pro at driving last year."

I get into the wheelchair and that feeling of déjà vu sweeps over me.

"I'll be back after lunch and we'll try six steps."

"Or ten."

"Ten it is." He raises his hand for a high five.

"Do you want to ride down to the Children's Activity Room?" Mom asks.

"No. It's full of blocks and dolls, remember?"

"They added a room with a TV, computers, books, stuff for older kids."

"Really?"

"Maybe your whining and complaining worked."

"Let's check it out." Mom pushes me out the door and down the hall. When we reached the door to the activity room, I shoo her away. "I'll take it from here. You go read a book or something." I roll myself in and look around. There's a boy in a wheelchair at a monitor playing Fortnite. I'm about to wheel toward him when I see the back of Martha's head in front of a computer.

"Martha?"

Chapter 17
Aluminum What?

"Ooze!" Martha is sitting in a wheelchair too, only her legs are sticking straight out and resting on metal plates. Her feet look mummified in layers of gauze bandages. We roll up to each other and bump fists. "Look," she says pointing to a PC monitor. "They have Fortnite."

Fortnite. I'm just not ready to go back yet. "What about Minecraft?"

"Only single player games. Can you teach me the basics of Fortnite?"

Just the basics. No leaderboards. "Sure." We roll up to a monitor. I put the keyboard in Martha's lap. Before starting I look at the clock. "Thirty minutes, then I want to get back to my mom."

"I want to get back to my mom, too."

"How is she?"

"She's getting better. She got pneumonia, but the docs say she'll be well enough to go home by the weekend."

"When can you go home?"

"They haven't said. You?"

"Don't know. Depends on how well my feet are doing. They want me to be able to stand and take some steps with a walker."

Her feet must be really bad. I can take steps now. "Did your mom's feet get burned?"

"Not at all. She had on leather boots with leather soles. So, for the next fire…"

"…Wear leather boots," we say together.

"How's Grimey?"

"Mom says he's doing good. So there are up to 100 players in each match. You want to be the last player standing or at least one of the last players standing at the end."

I walk Martha through a tutorial. For some reason, I'm just not feeling into it. "It's 11:30. Let's stop."

"We haven't even played a match yet."

"Matches can take up to 20-40 minutes or longer. You can't pause a match. It's play all the way through or get taken out."

"Will you come back after lunch?"

"I got PT after lunch, so maybe. I'm in room 310. Call me."

"I lost my phone."

"Me too, but you don't need it. Look." I point to an old

landline phone on the wall. "This place has a landline in every room. Just pick up the receiver and press 3-1-0 and the phone rings in my room."

"That's so cool. It's like a private server. I'm in room 321."

"Room 321, got it."

I wheel out of the Teen Lounge and go down the hall toward my room. As I get close, I hear voices. "Five!" I forget about my feet and jump up for a hug.

"Look at you, jumping around on burned feet. A real firefighter is in there," Five says as he points to my heart.

"Yeah, well, that hurt. I think I'll get off my feet for now and fight fires later." I slowly lower myself into the wheelchair.

"I'm proud of you, Ouzel. You were in deep trouble and you kept your wits. I know grown men who couldn't do that. I guess you can learn problem solving through those games of yours."

"I guess, but those games almost killed me."

"No, the games didn't force you to play again and again."

"I know. I chose to play."

"Why?"

"They're fun and I'm good at them."

"It sure does feel special to be good at something," Five agrees.

I nod my head. "And, I have fans. Gamers who follow me and want to be on my squad. I feel like I can't let them down, ya know?"

"Yeah, I hear ya. What are you going to do now… about gaming?"

"Nothing. I'm totally offline."

"Would you be up for helping me out with something?"

I point to my feet and shrug my shoulders. "Sure, but how?"

"Help me build a robot that can go into burning brush and spray powered aluminum hydroxide."

Build a robot! "What is that aluminum stuff?"

"Aluminum hydroxide. It's a chemical. When heat is added to it, as in flames, it changes into aluminum oxide."

"A chemical reaction. We studied those in science."

"Excellent. So, here's a question for you. Aluminum hydroxide to aluminum oxide, what's the difference?"

"The hydro—water!"

"Exactly, when the aluminum hydroxide meets the heat you get aluminum oxide and water. That water cools the flames…"

"And the fire goes out. The laws of combustion. I learned those from you."

"Now, the robot part. I thought you could use a project to keep you busy as you heal. And, I need robots to put out the smaller hot spots so the men can go where they are really needed. It's a win-win situation."

He's right. I do need to do something while I lie here. I don't even have a phone.

"I'll bring you a laptop for research, but no games—official firefighting business only. You in?"

"Yeah, I'm in." *I could use the internal parts of a remote-control car and then build a flame-resistant chassis.* "Could I build it in your workshop?" Five's face tells me the answer. "Is your ranch gone?"

Five tilts his open palm back and forth. "We lost the barns and the fences, but the house still stands. It's got smoke damage and it'll have to be gutted, but the concrete blocks and metal roof made it through."

"Did anybody die in the fire?"

"No, thank goodness. Zero deaths, three injured, and twelve structures burned. We were lucky."

"It doesn't feel lucky, Five. It feels...Well, it just hurts."

"I know, but the pain won't last. The memory, yes, but not the pain."

Chapter 18
The Surprise!

I'm getting discharged today. My feet are still tender, but I can walk slowly in shoes with a special cushy insert. Nurse Susan pushes my wheelchair down to the lobby. I could walk, but it's hospital regulations—something about liability insurance and stuff. Mom is walking beside me with her arms full of balloons and flowers. Dad is waiting in the circular drive with his truck.

"Thank you," I say to Nurse Susan as I hug her goodbye. "I know I wasn't the easiest patient."

"Come back to see me and let me know how you're doing."

"I will." *You and I both know I probably won't.*

"Ready to go home?" Dad asks.

"More than ready!" I know we're going to Uncle Coe's

ranch, but still it's better than the hospital. I'm excited to see the horses again, especially Grimey.

Mrs. Malkovich is home, too. Well, home as in a rental house in Chico. Martha needs to stay longer. I found out that third degree burns can be serious. Martha was wearing slip-on shoes with just a thin sole of synthetic rubber between her skin and the burning hot ground. Hardly any protection.

"Mom, the money in my bank account is safe, right?"

"Yes. The fire didn't affect the bank. Why?"

"I know that money is for college and maybe a car someday, but I want to take some out to buy Martha a pair of red leather western boots."

"I think that would be a perfect present." Mom looks at Dad and winks.

"Mom, we're just friends."

"We have a ways to drive. Why don't you lay back and rest?" Dad suggests.

"I'm too hyped. I've been in that hospital for eight days. I want to see stuff. And can we stop for burgers and a shake? Do you think the peppermint shakes are back?"

"You read my mind."

As we are waiting in the drive-through line, I see a poster advertising Peppermint Candy Stick shakes. *Yes!* It's weird getting excited over an ordinary thing like a milkshake. I'm actually excited about everything right now.

"Mom, is any station playing Christmas music?"

"Probably not until after Thanksgiving, but I have this." Mom holds up a worn CD of my first-grade holiday concert.

I remember hating this silly CD, but now it seems okay. "Sure, put it in."

I eat my double cheeseburger and slurp up my shake as I listen to squeaky voices sing *All I Want for Christmas is My Two Front Teeth*. I am happy.

"Dad looks at me through the rear-view mirror. "You finished back there?"

"Yeah, thanks. That was the best. Meal. Ever!"

"Maybe this will be even better."

Mom hands me a gift bag with a goofy turkey on it. "For me? Why?"

"Just open it."

I pull out a familiar rectangular box. "A new phone," I gasp.

"Just like the last one. Your contacts and apps should be set up."

I have an insane number of notifications and messages. Most of them are from gamers asking when I'm going to defend my position on the leaderboard or gloating because they just beat my score. They don't know what happened to me, or if they do, would they even care? They don't know me. They just know the legend of Mutant Blackbird. I swipe and delete those messages.

The rest of the messages are from people I know. They send get well memes or news from school. I even have an email from Mrs. Chen telling me to get better and not to worry about missed assignments. *Okay, I won't!*

I look up for a second from my phone. A truck pulling a long horse trailer is passing us. *Why is Dad letting this guy pass him?* A ping alerts me to a video message from Jake.

"Hey, Mutant! Heard you got sprung today. Call me. Fortnite match, tonight at 8." I think about checking our Discord leaderboard. *How far down did I go?* But the need just isn't there anymore. I don't really care about points right now.

I'm starting to get a headache. I've been looking down too much. I set down the phone and look out the window.

"Where are we going? This isn't the way to Uncle Coe's house."

"Check your phone. There's a new picture for you"

I wait for the pictures to load. The most recent one is of the barn. I don't understand. *Why would I want to be reminded of all we lost?* "Why is there a picture—"

"Enlarge it and look carefully."

The barn's sides are scorched black. The grass around the barn is charred black, too. *This picture was taken after the fire.*

Chapter 19
Going Home!

"The barn is still standing! How? I saw the gas tank explode."

"I can't explain it," Mom shakes her head. "The house is gone, but not the barn."

"So that's where we're going? Home?"

"That's where we're going."

"But this isn't Old Orchard…is it?"

"No, Old Orchard melted." Dad explains. "This is highway 13, the backway."

"It's not even burned around here."

"Fire makes its own unpredictable path. Up ahead here, you'll start to see the burned areas," Dad says as he points. Within minutes, I start to see blackened areas. The charred trees look like black skeletons waving their skinny arms.

"There's Five's place!" The sign over his driveway is untouched, but the two posts holding it up are charred black. The fields are black wastelands, too. I sit up straighter and lean forward so I can catch the first sight of our ranch. It should be right over this hill.

"It's hard to tell what's ours with the fence lines down," Mom says. She's right. Everything looks broken and burnt.

Dad turns onto our gravel road. The gravel is covered with a layer of ash. Only the crunch under the tires tells me that the gravel is still there. The corral fencing is totally gone, but Dad was right. The barn stands tall and unchanged except for some scorching along the walls and door. Behind the barn and to the right I see a new rail fence.

I get out of Dad's Jeep and limp slowly towards the back of the barn and the new fence. As I get closer, I see the back of a horse trailer. *That's the trailer that passed Dad.* Uncle Coe is backing Princess out on the ramp.

"Uncle Coe!" I call out as Mom swings open the new gate.

Mom takes Princess's lead. "You're home, girl. Let's get you in your stall." I follow Mom into the barn through the same doors I drove Madjiki's Jeep through. I squat down and put my hand on the barn's threshold. On the outside there is black, burnt earth. On the inside there is soft, sandy dirt.

"How? The doors were open, and the fire was right there," I tell Mom and Uncle Coe. "Look," I point to the melted, twisted metal of the lawnmower just outside of the barn door.

"Some things can't be explained, just accepted." Mom didn't seem surprised at all. "Where's Princess's blanket?"

"Probably at the bottom of Jake's pond." Mom didn't question that either.

"Grimey's in his stall," Uncle Cole says as he points.

I walk to Grimey's stall. He has his face in his oat bucket and his rump facing me. "Hey, old buddy, it's me." Grimey picks up his head and slowly turns around. He looks at me as he finishes chewing. I take a step closer, and he gives my head a kiss with his full horse lips. "I love you, too, Grimey." He turns back around and goes back to eating his meal as if the fire never happened.

"Ahhh!" Mom exclaims. "Ouzel, look." On the floor of the barn lies my framed baby picture. The glass is cracked and sooty, but the picture is okay.

"It must have fallen out of the box." Mom hugs the picture tightly.

With a chorus of whinnies, Amber and Jack trot into the barn. Their tails are up and they are nipping at each other's necks. "Go to bed," I tell them. Amber nods her head and snorts her approval as she backs into her stall.

"I'm outta here, guys. Need anything, just give me a call."

"Coe, you've helped so much. Thank you," Mom says as she hugs her big brother.

"Remember that extra sheet metal you talked about?" I ask Uncle Coe.

"It's leaning over there in the corner with that old remote controller race car."

"It's perfect, thanks!"

Dad walks in through the front barn doors. "Ouzel, you see this?" he asks as he points toward the ceiling. My eyes follow his finger.

"A loft?" There is a low, plywood ceiling over my head where there used to be open space up to the wooden rafters.

"Check it out. The stairs are over there."

I walk to the corner of the barn where there's a stairway built of fresh pine wood. *The smell of fresh wood is the best.* I want to take the stairs two at a time. Instead, I climb them one at a time like a fat baby. At the top is a large open room. On one side is a queen bed and a dresser. On the other side is a twin bed, highboy dresser and a desk with a green exercise ball. In between the two bedrooms sits a couch and low table with a TV.

"Where did you get this?" I ask Dad as he comes up the stairs.

"Five, Kee, Coe, and I built the loft. The furniture was either bought or donated."

"This is awesome. We have a home on our own land." I sit on the couch and look around. "What about a bathroom? And a kitchen?"

"You've heard of an outhouse? Well, we have a burned-out house. Come on, I'll show you."

We walk out of the barn and back into the stench of burned wood. This is the first time I've let myself look at the house. Two of the outside walls are still standing. The roof is gone. My old life is gone.

"Look, I made a path from the barn to the outhouse. I strung these Christmas lights so you can see at night." I follow Dad into the remains of the house. In the back corner, where the two standing walls meet, is the master bathroom. The toilet is still there. "We had to replace some of the PVC pipes, but we got it working. And, we have running water in the sink and shower."

The mirror is gone, as are the wooden cabinets around the sink, but the porcelain sink and pipes are still here.

"Mom bought a new shower curtain and I'll work at getting some sort of roof over it. We're camping in high style."

I can smell the new plastic odor from the shower curtain. It's a smell of the future among the burnt smell of the past.

"And for food?" I ask.

"That's the best part. Campfire food, plus there's a coffee maker and a microwave in the barn."

"Staying at Uncle Coe's would have been okay, but this is so much better. Thanks." I give Dad a hug.

"Don't thank me just yet. We have electricity, but no internet."

"That's okay. I don't need it. When can we start to rebuild the house for real?"

"That's up to the insurance people. We can't start to rebuild until we have that money. I'm hoping by spring."

My phone vibrates in my pocket. It takes me a moment to realize what it is. I haven't had to think about a phone for a while. "Hello? Oh, hi! Yeah, I made it home. You knew about the surprise! And you didn't tell me? It's great. I can't wait for you to see it. No, I can't. No internet here. For a while, I guess. It's not that bad. There's a lot I need to do on the robot. I'll see if I can come visit. Bye. I will. Oats, he likes oats. Bye."

"Martha?"

"Yeah," I answer. I feel my cheeks getting hot.

Mom climbs up the stairs carrying two fleece blankets. She throws one with big white snowflakes toward my head. "Here, it's going to be chilly up here with only that." She points to a space heater.

"Aren't those kind of dangerous? Do we have a smoke detector up here?"

"Yes, by the bed. We'll be careful with the space heater. No flammable fabrics within 10 feet, Mr. Firefighter."

We all sit down on the couch in our barn loft and snuggle under the fleece blankets. Mom tells the story about the day I was born and how they had to drive to the hospital in a snowstorm. I've heard the story a million times, but I still like it.

After the stories, I quietly say, "Mom, I know what my one thing is—my summit. It's people, taking care of people. Maybe I'll be a firefighter or a doctor or a physical therapist."

My phone vibrates again. I ignore it.

"Go on, check it," Mom urges. "People are worried about you."

"It's Jake. Let me text him back."

Can't play 2nite. Disconnected. Talk in the AM?

Dad is at the back of the TV. "What are you up to?"

"Just plugging this in." Dad holds up a dusty Wii console. "Another donation."

"Mom, you're going to love this. We can play bowling. This is the remote. Hold it like this."

"First, we have to make our Miis. Look, Kuli here is one with long dark hair."

"Where is one with gray hair for you," Mom teases.

"Can we make this one taller, for our Giraffe boy?"

Chapter 20
On Top Again

I've never been in a live competition like this before. Gaming is a competition, of course, but this is different. Our team's work is done. All I can do is wait for the judges to come to our display.

"We're next," Martha squeals. She nervously taps the toe of her red boot on the display table. The trifold board wobbles. The 'S' falls off the title, *Smokey the Firebot*. Martha jumps off her stool and slaps another piece of double-sided tape on the back of the fallen letter.

The California Science and Engineering Fair judges come up to our display. My mouth goes dry and my palms start to sweat. My voice cracks as I begin with our Introduction.

"When a major wildfire breaks out in California, it takes time and resources to assemble a full crew of firefighters from the Dispatch Center. What if Incident Commanders across the state were equipped with a roaming robot that could go into fields or forests and seek out heat in the form of embers or flames and then extinguish them? Our robot can get a head start on fire control before the crews arrive. Let me introduce you to Squad Five's Smokey the Firebot." The judges are scribbling notes as I talk.

Martha takes over and presents our Problem and Procedures sections. "We did not attempt to build a robot from scratch. We decided to use the tools and inventions that we already had. Well, we didn't have much of anything because we lost our homes in the wildfire in November, but we asked, and got donations from friends and family."

Martha is going off script. *What are you doing? We need to be all scientific.*

"So, we used a broadcast fertilizer spreader, a robotic lawnmower, a heat sensor from a smoke alarm, metal pole extenders, and a thermostat. If you would look at our board, I'll go over the specific steps."

The judges are leaning in to read our Procedures section. Martha is sticking with our practiced script, finally. *It's all good.* I pull at the knot at my neck to loosen my tie. *Breathe, it's almost over.*

"Next, Ouzel here will take you outside where we have Smokey the Firebot ready for a demonstration. I would go with you myself, but I am still on crutches because I had third degree burns on my left foot."

TMI Martha!

"Oh, you poor girl. I hope you'll be back on both feet soon."

Martha winks at me as I ask the judges to follow me. *Playing for the sympathy vote. We're gonna need it.*

Julio and Jake are outside by the parking lot. We made a sand track just for our demonstration. I nod to Julio, and he walks toward the two piles of dry twigs and branches. He flicks on the long neck lighter and lights one pile, then the other. Jake presses the power switch on Smokey. *Please start!*

Smokey begins to hum and rolls down the sand track. I can hear the judges whispering. Smokey stops, turns right and rolls over the first fire. The switch for the broadcaster comes on and the white powder spins out. The fire sizzles and goes out.

Jake begins his speech. "We just saw the aluminum hydroxide undergo a chemical reaction when exposed to heat. The products of that reaction—water and aluminum oxide—have extinguished the fire."

We could really win this! Smokey turns around and heads toward the second fire which has grown into a full campfire. *Too much fuel!* Smokey hums happily into the flames. I hear the click of the broadcaster and the flames get smaller...for a second. Flames leap up and surround Smokey. Jake grabs the fire extinguisher and puts out the flames.

Julio, Jake, and I just look at each other. "Game over," Jake mouths silently.

"Well done. Very impressive. A few glitches obviously, but overall, well done," says the judge with stars and comets on her shirt as she walks over to us to give us handshakes.

"Thank you." *They liked it?*

Another judge leans in and whispers in my ear. His garlic breath makes me want to turn away, but I don't. I lean in and listen to his words. "You learn more by what you get wrong. Keep at it."

We follow the judges back inside.

"How did it go?" Martha asks.

"I don't know. Smokey put out one fire and then burst into flames over the second one. Jake had to hose him down." I was afraid to look at Martha. What if she started to cry?

"Well, one worked, and one didn't. That's 50%. Pretty good for a new invention made by middle schoolers."

◆ ◆ ◆

After a fast food lunch we go back into the conference center for the award ceremony. The participants sit in one area and the parents sit in another. Jake, Julio, Martha, and I are squished together in a sea of middle schoolers.

Julio puts his finger on the side of his neck. "My heart is racing."

"Have you heard about robotic competitions?" Martha asks. "Maybe we can get a sponsor and start one at school? That way we could learn more and figure out how to make Smokey work like 100%."

"Good idea, Boots."

"Don't call me that."

"If you can call me Ooze, I can call you Boots."

"Deal," she says, sighing.

"Know what we are, Ouzel?" Asks Jake.

"What?"

"Casual, that's what. I haven't gamed in days."

"Yeah, I guess we are casuals. I'm not even on a leaderboard. I still want to play though. Sometimes."

"Well, yeah, me too, but I like what Martha said. A robotics team would be awesome."

"Shh, Jake, the judges," I say, pointing to the platform. The judges thank a mile-long list of people and sponsors and stuff. Finally, they start calling out awards for the middle school division. There are honorable mentions and then the places. Martha reaches out to hold my hand and Jake's. She squishes her eyes shut and starts to mumble in Hebrew.

Third Place is announced and it is not us.

Martha opens her eyes and says, "It's second. We have to get second. We messed up too much for first, so it has to be second."

"Or nothing," chimes in Julio. *That's what I'm thinking.*

"And 2nd place goes to Squad Five from Orchard Consolidated School for their Smokey the Firebot invention."

I can't process the words. *Us? Second?* Martha's squeals bring me back into the moment. I give a victory yell. Julio is already halfway to the platform. The crowd is clapping politely as I help Martha wobble to the platform.

As the judge with garlic breath hangs silver medals around our necks, I look out into the audience.

Dad is applauding louder than the folks around him, which would normally embarrass me but I'm too happy to care. Five is cheering and giving me an emphatic double thumbs-up. Mom's purse tumbles to the floor as she jumps up to clap. Seeing her beaming face I realize how much her smile looks like Madjiki's. *I know you're here with me, too.* First place is announced and the applause increases, but I feel like the celebration is just for us.

After the ceremony wraps up, people gradually make their way outside, stopping to talk and take photos. Mom pulls us all together for a group shot. As we lean in next to each other, with our medals glinting in the sunlight and the voices of excited students floating around us, I feel a fire inside of me. I haven't felt this way since my first match. We have to do this again next year and we've *got* to perfect our Firebot.

On the way home, I pull out my tablet.

"Playing a game?" Asks Mom as I put on my headphones.

"Thought about it, but I'm going to watch a video on programming robots."

"Want to play Rocket League tomorrow night?" Dad asks.

"Sure! I'll still own you, old man."

The End

Acknowledgments

Many thanks to the following people, without whom this story would still be locked in my head. Sandra O'Donnell, my book coach, agent, and friend. The team at Blackbird & Birch, thank you for turning my ragged manuscript into the finished work. Emily Ullrich, illustrator extraordinaire, your illustrations bring my story to life. My writing tribe – Angela Blount, Sarah Belanger Demaneuf, Beth Skarupa, Liz Bergquist, and Judd Vowell, thank you for reading, directing and encouraging. My family, thank you for reading multiple drafts and being my cheerleaders. Beta readers Philip and Joe, thank you for your meticulousness and honesty. And finally, much gratitude to Ouzal – the original blackbird.

About the Author

Mary Lee Soop is a National Board–Certified Teacher in Middle Grades reading and writing, thriving on 30 years of grade school energy and mayhem. She lives in Huntsville, Alabama with her husband and two Shetland Sheepdogs as she writes middle-grade fiction. Wildfire Ridge is her debut middle grade novel. For more information visit www.maryleesoop.com

About the Illustrator

Emily Ullrich is an artist and illustrator born and raised in Austin, Texas who has pursued art in many forms, from mural painting to scientific illustration. Emily currently resides in Culver City, California, where she loves to go on nature walks and play video games. For more information visit www.ekullrich.carbonmade.com

Guided Reading Questions

Chapter 1

1. What did you learn about Ouzel and Martha in this chapter? Tell five things you know about each of them.
2. What does "mutant" mean?
3. Would you be friends with Ouzel? Explain why or why not.

Chapter 2

1. Why does Martha come over to Ouzel's house?
2. What is a yearling?
3. Why does Grimey stare at the road?
4. Can you put your finger on the sentence that foreshadows what will happen in the future?
5. How did Five get his name?

Chapter 3

1. At the beginning of the chapter, why does Ouzel feel anxious?
2. What is Kuli, Ouzel's mom, worried about?
3. Ouzel grabs three items to put in the cardboard box in case the family has to evacuate. What three things would you grab from your room?
4. Why doesn't Ouzel hear his phone alarm?
5. How does winning a game make you feel?

Chapter 4

1. What happens that tells you about Ouzel's character?
2. This chapter refers back to something told in Chapter 1. Why was Ouzel in the hospital last year?
3. What are pyrocumulus clouds?
4. Put your finger on a sentence that makes your heart beat faster.
5. Why does Martha drop out of the game?
6. What mistake does Ouzel make?

Chapter 5

1. What does this mean— "Amber is afraid of sounds that I can't hear"?
2. Share one good idea that Ouzel learned from video games.
3. Why are Ouzel's lips too dry to whistle?
4. What does it mean to canter?
5. Where do you think Princess goes?

Chapter 6

1. Does Ouzel choose wisely? Why or why not?
2. What kind of tight spots has Ouzel been in before?
3. What is a mentor? Who is Ouzel's mentor in this chapter?
4. Explain Ouzel's feelings when he says, "I've lost."

Chapter 7

1. What is a tack closet?

2. Who is Ouzel's mentor in this chapter?
3. Was Ouzel right to choose the Jeep over the four-wheeler?
4. Some things had to happens before Ouzel could drive the Jeep—cause and effect. Ouzel had to _____ before he could drive the Jeep. Think of three events to fill in the blank.

Chapter 8

1. How does being a gamer help Ouzel in this chapter?
2. What skills have you learned by playing video games?
3. Which would Ouzel say is more exciting—real life or a video game?

Chapter 9

1. Five believes that Ouzel will be okay, so Ouzel believes it too. Why is encouragement so powerful?
2. Did it surprise you that Ouzel stopped to save a wild hare?
3. Search for the meaning of an idiom. Can you find an example of an idiom in this chapter?

Chapter 10

1. Why does Martha think that Ouzel's dad is driving the Jeep?
2. How do you think Grimey got to the pond?
3. What does the word catalyst mean? What is the catalyst for getting Martha and her mother to run through the flames to the pond?

Chapter 11

1. Were Ouzel's words and actions disrespectful to Mrs. Malkovich? Why or why not?
2. What do you think are more dangerous—embers or flames?
3. How can a fire jump over water?

Chapter 12

1. When you're a kid, there are times when you want the adults in your life to leave you alone, and then other times when you want them to take charge. Why is that? What are some things that you are glad your parents handle?
2. Why does Martha sink under the water?
3. Do you think Ouzel really sees Madjiki?
4. Search for a picture of a horse's hoof. Can you locate the frog?
5. What do you think Mrs. Malkovich sees when she looks at Martha's feet? Why doesn't she tell Martha?

Chapter 13

1. What is an asphalt road made of? Can it melt in a fire?
2. What does smoke do to your lungs?
3. How does Ouzel know so much about fire and smoke?
4. Riding out of the fire on Grimey is the lowest point of the ordeal for Ouzel. Why?

Chapter 14

1. How can an old horse jump over the fire line? Hint—search the word adrenaline.
2. Where did the horses go? Do you think they had been there before?
3. Why won't Five let Ouzal show him where Martha and her mom are waiting?
4. Which is more life threatening—burned feet or smoke damaged lungs?

Chapter 15

1. Why does Ouzel's mom say, "Welcome back"?
2. Why does Ouzel feel guilty?
3. Why is Ouzel surprised that he is his mom's summit? Do you think a child can understand how much their parent's love them?
4. Can you always believe what your friends say? How do rumors get started?

Chapter 16

1. The human body is amazing! Search catheter and muscle atrophy. Why is standing hard for Ouzel?
2. How are laughing and crying similar?
3. What is Déjà vu?

Chapter 17

1. Why doesn't Ouzel want to play Fortnite?
2. It feels good to do something well! What are you good at?
3. Science is about understanding our world. What is an element? What is a chemical reaction?
4. What did Five give Ouzal?

Chapter 18

1. Why doesn't Martha get discharged from the hospital when Ouzel does?
2. Research the word synthetic. What's the difference between synthetic leather and real leather?
3. Why does a regular hamburger and milkshake taste so good to Ouzel?
4. Ouzel gets a new phone. He is a thirteen-year-old seventh grader. Do you think he is too young for his own phone? What is good about having a phone of your own? What is bad?

Chapter 19

1. How can fire hop around and leave some areas untouched?
2. Ouzel's house is gone, but he is home. What does home mean to you?
3. What is Ouzel's summit?

Chapter 20

1. Which would make you more nervous—a live, in-person competition or a virtual one?
2. Why didn't Squad Five win first place?
3. How does Ouzel handle the failure of the robot?
4. What life lesson did Ouzel learn from the wildfire? Did he share this lesson with others?
5. Is Ouzel a hero?

Made in the USA
Coppell, TX
02 March 2022

74222323R00085